Neale Sourna's
North Coast Academies' Journal 1

The Compilation of

Neale Sourna's
North Coast Academies' Diary
Volumes 1-3

by
Neale Sourna

Cleveland OH USA

Copyright © 2010 by Neale Sourna

Print ISBNs: 978-0-9741950-4-9 / 0-9741950-4-9

In this compilation, there has been reparagraphing—for ease of reading—and the occasional correction or change of a word or minor punctuation from the original published issues; plus, the individual forewards were deleted to maintain uninterrupted joy of storytelling; but, nothing else has been changed in context or story. —Love, Neale

August 2010

Published by

PIE: *Perception* Is *Everything*™
12600 Rockside RD Box 192
Cleveland OH 44125 USA

www.PIE-PerceptionIsEverything.com
www.PIE.Percept.com
www.Neale-Sourna.com

Table of Contents

Neale Sourna's
North Coast Academies' Diary

Laila: Cozy With Daddy *[7857 words]*

An Adult Fiction Compiled by

Neale Sourna

Brainy, multiracial, private school virgin, Laila Mariah Deever, chooses to seduce her handsome, middle-aged stepfather, Ross, for her first incestuous, cherry-picking fuck.

This fiction includes budding valedictorian Laila's *first* wet dream, featuring lesbian wet cunnilingus; her *first* voyeurism with her *first* masturbation; her *first* brief taste of cum and fatherly *first* fingerfuck; her *first* dirty talk; and most definitely her very *first* all out father-daughter fuck.

Whoo! Those overachievers.

ISBN: 0-9741950-5-7
ISSN 1553-8656
Volume 1, Issue 1

May 2006

Laila: Cozy with Daddy
by
Neale Sourna

Alice was doing adult stuff Daddy says I'm not to do with boys. Or girls. Or even with myself, alone. Stuff he knows some kids my age do, "wh-which isn't w-wrong, exactly, Laila," is how he barely puts it, before refusing to discuss it further, except to say, "You can ask me anything, Laila.

"About . . . about s-sex. I don't want others teaching you the wrong things. It should be m-me tea — ."

That's when he lately always gulps, and then bites his lips shut. Daddy doesn't want to think of me, or anyone else, touching me, like that, but I'm not completely certain why.

Anyway, I was alone with Alice, my best friend, who swears she doesn't look like a teenaged version of that plump, spunky Dixie Chick — *but she does.*

We were alone in the humid girls' locker room at school, and Alice was lying on a red towel over the blond wood bench by our lockers, stark naked — creamy blue white skin against red terry cloth. I repeat; stark naked, except for white gym socks, white Reeboks®, and her sparkling gold Star of David.

She's not exactly Jewish, she just wears it. Don't ask.

Alice was touching herself, and writhing and moaning, which seemed way interesting and well inviting, especially with her being so bold about it, so I looked closer, smelling her, as she opened her round, white thighs wider.

As the dark red brown, painted nails of her pale fingers disappeared in and out, in and out, covered in glistening, dripping wet, muskiness.

As she parted the soaked platinum blond, curly pubes, she pulled back on her hairy lips down there and revealed flushed, vulnerable, deep rose pink—.

J. H.! I couldn't bear it.

I dove. I actually dove in and licked Alice's juicy pussy, like a greedy little pig and loved it!

She moaned louder, writhing and grinding hot and wet against my face, smothering me in plump, musky flesh, and tart juice, juice, and more juice, flowing like a river.

I kept getting it in my nose, but I couldn't stop lapping at her and she kept moaning, as I nipped and pinched with my lips and she moaned louder.

I poked my tongue hard inside her—.

That's when I felt him. I felt my big, naked Daddy behind me, his hot flesh pressed stone hard against my own naked, dripping wet-showered skin. He was entering me, filling me with his hard, thick—.

Fuck!!

Sorry. Language.

My stupid alarm abruptly woke my burning brain, but my body remained hot, sweaty, and . . . slippery, as I started my school day.

As you know, I'm Laila. Laila Mariah Deever. What you don't know is that I'm multiracial. Isn't everybody?

I'm African, Native, and European American with creamy tan skin, shoulder length, medium deep dark auburn, wavy hair, and large root beer brown eyes with gold wire frames [*I'm nearsighted and can't stand contacts, besides I look smart as all hell in specs.*].

Almost 5'3" and 104-ish lbs.

Straight A's and I'm the preferred Valedictorian frontrunner, no matter what that snot Amy says.

My Daddy, Ross Martin Deever, makes certain I'm protected.

He specifically chose and switched me from my old private school way back in the day to a more exclusive private girl's academy, co-affiliated as part of four private schools; a coed middle school; a girls' high school and a boys' high school which share some facilities; and a super, exclusive college nearby.

All with the same name, only the buildings and the grades change. So, I've gone there like forever, and pretty much feel like I own the place, and run the place.

Which I do, of course. But shush, don't tell anyone.

Nevertheless, my ensured safety in the public community is paramount at home, too. Daddy's gotten v-chips for our TVs and cable and a software cop for my computer and his, but I've seen a man's thick, hard naked cock, anyway.

Two cocks, to be more precise.

"Cocks," that's what Alice and her mom calls them. Daddy doesn't think I know that kind of language, or use it, so if you tell him that I do, adult or student, I will cut you from the social herd and make you most extremely, *extremely* sorry.

Anyway, the prettiest one—*I can say "pretty," can't I?*—the prettiest cock, the one particular cock I couldn't take my eyes off, was my own Daddy's.

Every time I remember it, my pussy entirely aches and drives me insanely mad, which is what I told Alice, without telling her *exactly* whose cock it was. Let's face it, most people don't understand that kind of thing, especially since Freud helped make everything all screwed up and deviated.

I haven't fully read Freud, y'know; I'm smart, but there is a limit to terminal dullness, even for me. But compulsive, chain-smoking, phallic cigar-sucking Freud-guy said that so many of his *fe*-male clients talked about, well, doing it with their fathers, because that's what they *imagined* and *really wanted,* but tried to deny.

"Penis envy" and all that crap?

Some contemporary therapists recently went back over and all through his patient records and found F-guy was seriously remiss in accepting what all those young teen women had said, because he was of the old school, y'know, the one that says that *all* women are deviants who lie?

So, F-guy never believed the girls when they'd said their fathers were pulling up their petticoats and doing them.

Many if not most of F-guy's clients weren't into that, and not happy about it at all; or at least they were heavily conflicted about it, whether they liked it or not, since society at large says it's a big, fat no-no.

Anyway, back to me, and because *this* girl's got to talk to her best girl, Alice, about such things and because, well, I'm basically, sinfully honest and sometimes I just forget and get careless enough to blurt things out.

To cover, I told Alice the cocks I'd seen were the Crosses', the very deliciously of age to sexually rage, fraternal twins, Tyb and Tad; short for Tybalt *(like in "Romeo and Juliet")* and Thaddeus.

I think that one's a family name.

Cockwise, I wouldn't know for certain, about either of them, so, for Alice's sake, since they live right across the restricted, wide boulevard from Daddy and me, I just made it up, as I enthusiastically gushed all orgasmic about "Tibby's" pretty cock.

"Laila! Alice!"

Daddy'd overheard part of what we'd said. He walks softly, like a traditional Native American hunting or something, which makes it impossible, by sound, to always tell where he is.

He was directly behind us, as Alice and I lay on our stomachs across my bed; and "nasty girl" words, especially around me, let alone *from* me, makes Daddy absolutely uncomfortable.

So, no more c-words, for now.

Hiding things from my Daddy can also be a problem, since, unlike some negligent parents I know, he actually checks up on me and stuff; not that I have much I want to hide from him. And not like he's all psycho about it but, as he says it, he's a "constant man," and is constantly vigilant about me.

He, in fact, hasn't touched another woman since he and Momma married, despite tons of North Coast City (NCC), Ohio, America,

USA parents, school staff types, and oversexed classmates of mine trying.

Of both sexes.

For god's sake, the things I've heard people who want my Daddy naked say about him. Not fit for a growing girl's ears, I tell you.

But, I should explain more.

Well, back in the day, Momma got herself pregnant, and he stood by her and married her and was there when I was born—*the first man to ever hold me*.

He works here, at home, at his metalsmith's design workshop, which is attached to the house, but faces the private street behind and down the little wooded hill.

His display shop and factory's across town, and run by his half brother, Stan.

Daddy designs and, like a blacksmith of yore—*now there's a lovely word I normally never get to use*—he builds pricey, exquisite, and exclusive blade and ancient armaments; y'know, swords, crossbows, and stuff, for private owners and theatrical types; stage and film—think "Lord of the Rings."

He also contracts to companies that sell to people who play at being knights, "Highlander" immortals, and "Conan: The Barbarian" or "Xena: Warrior Princess," and the like.

No comment. I've been to a convention or two. Nice people as a whole, but seriously *no comment*.

Every day, Daddy drops me at school then picks me up afterward, and at Tai Chi and ballet, or wherever.

For my safety.

All my friends, especially Alice, are entirely envious and are in complete, total love with him. And masturbate thinking of him.

Yes, they have told me this.

I understand though. Gross, but I understand.

Let's face it. My Daddy Ross is gorgeous.

Not quite classic handsome, his face is far *too interesting* for that, but it's a great and fantastic face with lots of sexy good structure and character in it; with the most perfect, mixed silver and black wavy, curly, longish hair; tiny laugh crinkles; and a superdashing, black mustache and beard, that's kind of goatee-ish.

A total cavalier.

And he "has a stunning body that's hard to get out off your mind, the kind to make you certain you want to do outrageous sin, day and night, to yourself and to him," per direct quote from Alice.

I completely agree.

And, I completely belong to him, of course.

He's my *real* Dad, no matter what Momma and that counterfeit birth certificate she showed me says.

I've seen the other papers, too.

He legally adopted me and loves me, with every word, glance, and gesture.

Genetic Sperm Dad, however, is a total ass wipe. Period.

She takes me, kicking and screaming, to see him every now and then, just to make my Daddy all angry.

Momma dated them both, simultaneously, before I was born. Ew! and Slutty!

The really creepy thing is that they kinda look like brothers, more so than he and Uncle Stan, explaining why people often think Daddy Ross is my genetic dad.

"Kitten?"

My Daddy calls me "Kitten" or "Baby"; and when in a mood to be an annoying tease, for his amusement alone not mine he calls me "Baby Halle," 'cause he says I look like the actress.

I don't really think so, must be the smart girl next door look thing or something, but she's multiracial, too, and is like "the most beautiful woman in the world," or something, right?

Which isn't all bad, I guess.

And she's like this utter gorgeous – guy – with – a – sexy – cool - job magnet.

Anyway, I most certainly hope I get tits like hers one day, 'cause, I look in the mirror and all I see are these Golden Delicious, apple-sized, baby breasts, which make me look like I'm about fourteen and a half. A *mature* and *brainy* . . . fourteen and a half. *(Place sigh here.)*

Daddy says he likes that I still look this way, like maybe it'll keep the old creeps away.

I don't think so, if the old ganders on the street or in the stores with their hands stuffed deep center of their greasy front pockets are a clue, because my looks certainly are no Kryptonite to creepy old tweedy teachers either, and besides my Daddy doesn't like the young boy creeps either.

Tibby and Tad from across the street were utterly banned from our house, since that closet game they both were teaching me.

Alice, who knows tons of useful stuff, says looking brainy babyish in gold wireframes doesn't matter, that I'm still "hot," and that all the boys say so; some of the girls, too, which is not something I'm sure, yet, that I wanted to know.

I do have great legs and a great butt from all the dancing and athletics. Everyone says that, but, unfortunately, I "have to wait for the rest," Momma, the Invisible Woman, says.

What I'd like to know is, why is it that a person, namely me, always has to "wait until you're of the proper age" and stuff?

What is the "proper age" for doing adult things, anyway?

Oh, yeah, *she* finally came home, a few weeks back, after Daddy'd argued with her on the phone in these tense, hissing whispers I wasn't supposed to overhear. Momma's got this traveling, glory job she adores more than anything, more than Daddy. Or me, so–.

"Fuck her." Damn! I bet he heard me. I'm not supposed to curse.

"Kitten, come here. It's okay. Don't cry."

She'd left, *again*. On my "special" birthday. Daddy says all my birthdays are special, but most especially this one. Momma doesn't seem to think so; she hates it every time I have another one.

Myself, I don't get the whole birthday thingy, especially any of those that mark the ultimate old enough to legally AND morally do whatever you want to "proper age."

Is the proper number a Jewish thirteen, a driving sixteen, a voting eighteen, or drinking twenty-one?

Which is it, already?

Pick ONE.

The SAME ONE, please.

Or, better yet, let me choose.

Oddly, at *no time* are you ever "old enough" to touch your own stuff. Or at least in my research I have yet to find a "legal or moral" standard of any kind mentioning it.

Perhaps, I missed it.

Anyway, that ultimate "old enough" magic number has also been as low as ten or eight, or less, depending on the country, the sex of the person, and the time period.

Teachers, especially Dean Prude *(Yes, it's her "official" nickname.)*, hates it when I bring this one up in class.

And don't get me started on those tricky ancient Hammurabi Code of Laws we were assigned to study; the oldest laws documented on the planet.

One says a rich guy putting his thing in his daughter gets banished, while another says the same rich guy caught thinging his own mother *(after dad's been thinging her — yes, it actually says that)*, well, both the son and mom get burned to a crisp.

Owy! And not fair.

But, as my academic advisor says, I digress.

Back to *my* life, and who I'm choosing to be my first. Y'know "my first" first. And I don't mean those lovely half-breeds Tyb or Tad. Or yummy Yune the delicious Korean.

It's like this.

Dear old Momma's never around, and I can't say I totally miss her or anything, but it does mean my Daddy's alone, except for me, so I was still standing there—*remember, I was crying, like a foolish idiot*—after my party, long after she'd Indy 500ed away, leaving me selfishly bawling at full Niagara Falls, for what reason I don't know.

Daddy came up behind me, turned me around, and held me tight to him.

That's all.

God, I *love* his gentle kisses, sweet mustachioed, soft bearded kisses; on my hair, cheek, and forehead kisses. Big, juicy, bear hugs against his strong, hard body. God, he smells and feels so good!

Better than boys who hug me.

They're not supposed to, he doesn't like it, but it feels good when the right ones do.

Just think of it as scientific research I need to know. That's what I'm telling him if, well, if he asks.

Y'know, my moms, she-devil that she is; didn't even sleep with him!! Her own legal husband. How could she be like that? What is the point of being married?!

Stan, my step half uncle, says Daddy should get an official separation. I think a divorce would make better sense, 'cause she's not up to her motherly and wifely duties.

I'm not just hatin' on her.

It's just . . . .

Y'know, way back in the long ago, seeing them cuddle, then later hearing them in their room, doing whatever grownups do alone, when they play together, always made me feel safe and loved. And hopeful, that one day I'd play those same fun games, whatever they were, with my own husband, who'd be just like Daddy.

Now, his broad chest rose under my childish, plump cheek; rising and falling in a deep, rumbly sigh, his chin resting on the crown of my head.

Completely, utterly nice.

"My Little Kitten's special birthday, I don't know what I'll do, now. You're all grown up."

"'Grown'?" I giggled, "In my starched, white camp shirts and itchy, herringbone plaid uniform skirt?"

That made him laugh, a little nervously, but he laughed.

At least our silly school uniform has a solid colored, no pattern jacket.

The phone rang and rang then, and neither of us got it, as it rolled over to voicemail; because lately all sorts of icky, childish boys keep nagging me about attending Homecoming and the Winter Dance, not to mention the early comers for the Spring Fling and class Prom, too, all trying to get an invitation in with me before Yune or Tyb.

I like boys, mind you, a lot really, but what I'm certain I need from a man, even well-developed Yune and Tibby, I know they don't have.

Plus, I've never really dated, anyway, Daddy doesn't approve, he says boys'll teach me "bad things, too soon."

Like kissing and groping in closets, with fraternal twins Tyb and Tad.

For instance, a lot of the kids have hotel rooms booked for ALL those school event date nights, including the before mentioned libidinous Cross Boys, whose naughty reputation is quite verifiable, I assure you.

Their mom the PAEB [Parents Education Advisory Board] Queen herself is footing the bill for that one, against their dad's wishes. Their mom spoils them rotten. But it's a kinda nice rotten.

Alice says I like their rottenness because I'm spoiled a little rotten myself, by my Daddy.

Anyway, even the poorer kids, who can't afford rooms, are pooling their cash and renting stretch limos or a group room to grope and play in.

It's a waste of money, and vile and disgusting, too.

No. I'm not a prude.

I mean doing it on high traffic, public used surfaces?

Let Adrian "Monk" or "CSI: Crime Scene Investigation" take a look at that with a black light.

YYYuck!

Sorry, I digressed, again. I'll stop it, really.

Daddy's squeezing me so tight.

Daddy was still comforting me, as if he didn't need a huge hug himself, too, but I stood still as marble, though, 'cause he was bulging—*his cock, I mean*—right against my belly making me feel achy below and all hot, humid, and slick between my thighs.

It's a thing a girl notices. A thick, hardening cock pressing into your belly?

Even a daughter notices.

But is it really wrong to, y'know, notice?

And to like it? A lot.

I could lie and be all PC, but I won't. I want my Daddy's beautiful cock.

* * * *

We had dinner and stayed over at his brother Stan's. The half brother.

My half step cousin, Taffy, who's a few months older than me, had fallen asleep, once we'd stopped talking and giggling; intense red curls, just like her father's, except without that shock of silver white he has, all in her green blue eyes with the long red lashes lying against cream toned, fresh scrubbed skin.

The noisy hot tub under her open window'd lulled her out immediately.

Silly wench was like that at camp too, could sleep through a tornado. The tub noise kept me awake.

Plus, I was trying to overhear, as Uncle Stan and Daddy talked about Momma being "gone all the time," and Daddy asking Uncle Stan about whether he thought I was "old enough" to something *something*.

"Old enough" for what I couldn't hear.

Then it happened.

Daddy got out, to get a beer, and there it was, dangling between his hard, athletic and hairy thighs, dripping torrents of water, a black patch of hair at its root.

He was entirely, most definitely, *definitely* naked!

So was my uncle!

Two cocks!! Nads too!

As the boys at school call them. Fuzzy red-haired ones, fuzzy black-hai- . . . .

Daddy stretched the full length of his powerful body, entirely on display within the high wall enclosed backyard, before grabbing a beer, then returning back to the tub.

He has a really great ass. Other's'd said so, but now I *really* got it.

Back and front.

I squeezed my thighs tight together, until my hip joints hurt, watching, for the first time, the two most important men in my life sitting naked on the tub's edge.

Uncle Stan came inside to bed, while Daddy stayed, dangling his legs up to the knee in the bubbly water; so I saw him touch it.

I reached into my pink cotton panties, so I could do like Alice'd done in my dream, touching my dark auburn hairy slot. It was swollen and wet and needing to be touched.

Touching myself felt good.

I rubbed myself wetter, for the first time ever, fingers slick and musky, while I watched Daddy leisurely stroke himself.

My Daddy's cock hardened and rose up utterly thick and tall. I'd never seen anything like that before! Not in full view. Just PBS type vids where it's a heat sensitive photo in unnatural human colors, of a cock hardening and standing, but it's not a *real* view, eye to naked flesh.

Our sex non-education is a total joke.

School's way too strict, Dean Prude and the so-called city fathers and mothers, like Mr. and Mrs. Cross.

I need to know this!

About cocks!

Daddy wasn't stuttering, all embarrassed, now; he was showing me, teaching me — *like he'd promised* — about sex, with his fantastic, big cock in both hands.

Y'know, I need to say, I really do love the word "cock," it is such an explosive and powerful word, filling one's mouth with so much . . . potential.

Daddy stroked the length of it, sometimes rubbing its fat head, and massaging his testicles, I mean nads, too.

I never knew men did that.

No one tells you anything truly useful.

Like I'll ever need the Monroe Doctrine and iambic pentameter on a daily basis.

Taffy abruptly turned over, sticking a long, bare leg out from under the covers, frightening me all to Hell, before realizing she was still asleep.

So, I resettled, pulled off my panties, stuffed them under my fat pillow, then, as I watched him, I tried slipping a finger inside me, like Alice says she does, like she did in my dream, as I pretended my nail polish free finger was Daddy's long, fat cock; but it hurt, my finger hurt me.

I was too tight.

No wonder nearly every girl says the first time is way not great, which means the movies and novels lie, really big time.

Or they leave out something crucial like Sex Ed class obviously has.

I needed, I'm not certain what I needed, as I went back to rubbing and pressing harder, because it felt so good and was feeling even more better.

Daddy was making faint sounds, as his hands made furious motions.

I tried to match and feel what he felt, but rubbing too hard hurt, though I almost felt . . . something *really great*, but lost it. I stupidly just couldn't get it right.

Managed to fog my glasses, though. I stoppe—.

Did he say my name?!

His stiff, heavy cock suddenly spurted, just then.

I'd always thought Alice lied, saying a man's stuff was "cream," like food—*Redi-Whip® in a kielbasa shaped can*—but Daddy's "cream" jetted out across the water, looking like warm, sweet, tasty Vanilla ice cream, frothing on the bubbles, foaming together, as he threw back his head, making odd faces, panting, and milking out more and more, until finally slowing and stopping.

His cock slowly relaxed and softened and curved down to rest along his thigh.

I felt different but I hadn't cum. Not by what Alice describes.

I was intruding anyway; he was having private adult time.

I shouldn't have been watching him; still I couldn't stop wondering, while wiping my fingers dry on my pink, cotton panties, how hard his big cock might feel in my small palm, if all his thickness would actually fit deep inside me, and what my Daddy's warm, fresh cream truly tasted like.

Sweet like warm vanilla ice cream or . . . ?

Alice swears cum is salty, or at least her exboyfriend's is.

I ducked out of sight when Daddy looked straight at Taffy's window.

* * * *

Daddy'd had something on his mind, since Uncle Stan's and my birthday party, too; not Momma, she wouldn't be back anytime soon, she'd made that clear when he'd called, begging her to come, in the first place, and she'd made it *very* clear again when she left after my party.

My winning English Lit Comp scholarship essay meant absolutely nothing to her, either.

They needed her.

She was the expert.

Ms. Fix-It-All-At-Work-But-Never-Comes-Home. Fine. We can take care of each other, without her.

"Fuck her."

"What's that, Kitten?"

"N-Nothing, Daddy." I know he'd heard me, even over the TV, but'd decided to let it go. He does that sometimes; he says, "Kids need to be kids, childish one minute, grownup the next."

He'd been watching me, I smiled, sheepish, his little girl caught being grownup. And foulmouthed.

We were home alone, as usual; having had dinner alone together, as usual. He was still in his robe, he'd taken an uncharacteristically long shower, after being all restless and tense about something all day, but he was plainly still restless and tense, as he stared oddly at me, before abruptly getting up and disappearing into his room.

It was time, I thought, before I chickened out.

A short bath.

Thick, wavy, shoulder length, medium dark auburn hair up, held by an antique, gold French comb he'd given me.

Gold wire framed glasses put away, and large, root beer brown eyes uncovered and a bit unfocused—I'm not totally blind or any-thing, and can do without them for the moment.

I moisturized my soft cream tan skin with original Jergens® lotion with its classic cherry-almond scent, which he likes.

I slipped into new clothes I'd bought with my saved allowance.

No makeup, he doesn't like me in makeup.

I was so nervous, but committed, and biting my lip. I stopped it, silly, childish habit.

I can do this; I'm old enough and smart enough to do this.

When I want something; to learn something, do something, I ana-lyze it, prepare for it, and put my full heart, put all of me into it. I'd read everything I could get my hands on.

I was ready, all new, "So Fresh and So Clean," like my Outkast CD DVD says. I knocked and entered.

Daddy was sitting on the edge of his and Momm- . . . on *his* bed, in nothing but his thick, white terry cloth robe still, his head in his hands, kind of like that statue of The Thinker. He sat bolt upright when I came in.

"What's the matter, Kitten?" His voice was tight, strained.

"I-I . . . ."

I'd practiced all kinds of clever things to say and couldn't manage one, so I just slid off my fuzzy, old, pink chenille robe with the teddy bear on the bottom.

Forgot to get a cool, grown up looking wrap.

He didn't say anything, but his eyes widened, a lot.

He sort of seemed to stop breathing, while staring at my new bright white, lace pushup bra [*Finally, decent, nearly "indecent" cleavage!*] and matching lace, Tanga boy panties; cut straight across, low on the hip, with just a hint of rounded butt cheek peeking. He pulled his robe tighter and sat straighter.

"Laila, what's *this*?"

He sounded angry, and his eyes were terrible. I bit my lip again, but he was waiting for an answer.

"I-I b-bought it, to wear. For you, Daddy."

He stared at me, kept staring at me, as if he were angry, so I quickly kissed him full on the lips, then waited for storm or sunshine. Neither came.

I kissed my Daddy again, taking more time to feel his lips warm against mine, the softness of his wonderful beard and mustache; he sighed and kissed back a little, before groaning and gently, but definitely, pushing me away.

I didn't like that, but hoped I could change his mind, yet.

"Laila, this isn't—."

I fumbled open the front hook of my itchy bra, and let it fall off. I then stupidly scratched my too pert, immature breasts — damn itchy lace.

Why my body isn't as mature outside as it feels inside, or as mature as my mind, is grossly unfair, Mother Nature.

My cream tan boobs just sat there, as unspectacular as fresh apples topped with round, walnut brown tips. Sorry, I think of food sometimes, when I'm real nervous.

I took his hand, so beautiful and skilled, and put his big, hard palm on me, on my bare breast; he didn't resist, but he didn't move, either, while his cock rose, tenting his robe and my wide, puffy aureoles tightened, until my nipples, hardened to the size of hard little, sweet raisins against his palm.

How strange.

It felt like he was pulling on my pussy through my breasts. Touching one part of me and reaching another, from the inside me.

His voice sounded odd, too. Thicker, like he was dazed.

"Laila, Baby, are you certain?"

I nodded, too terrified to speak, but stubborn to have my way, to have my Daddy; then I was afraid a nod wasn't enough.

"Yes, Daddy. Please?"

I slowly sat on his lap, gently squishing right up on his delicious, hardening lump and softly kissed him again.

He kneaded, pinched, and squeezed my little breasts and nipples, sending sharp, fiery chills through me, from tit to crotch, while he gently bit my lips, before sliding his long, hard, big tongue into my mouth.

I'd never been kissed like that; kissed a little, before he'd thrown Tyb and Tad out, but not like —!

My gold comb fell from my thick hair, as my Daddy laid me back on his bed, his hot mouth and breath burning me, as he replaced pinching fingertips with warm lips and hot tongue that made both my nipples tug on my pussy and drive me madly crazy.

My nipples tightened hard, making my crotch ache, like a mouth sucking without anything to suck on, at least not yet.

So sensitive. God, I never knew my tits, my everything could feel so —.

"Oh!"

Dean Prude, in Sex Ed'd, never mentioned this. Left out all the useful stuff, completely.

My Daddy stopped!

He stared at me and I couldn't read his expression. I can always read his expressions.

"D-Did I do something w-wrong, Daddy?"

I was panting, like I'd been running, while lying on his bed flat on my back!

"Laila, have you been like this, with any boy, or girl, I don't know about?"

"No!"

"You have a toy, Laila? Do you have a sex toy you've used, and hidden from me?"

Alice and her mom had those; stunned, I just bucked my eyes wide and shook my head, like a silly little, clueless baby.

He nodded, pleased with my answers, then shed his robe. J. H.! He was much more huge up naked close. My childish eyes must've been saucers.

"Don't worry about my size, Kitten. You'll fit me perfectly, once I get you ready. Jesus, Little Baby, you know, you've been on my mind, every moment, awake and asleep, since you watched me jack off at Stan's."

Gosh, he *had* called my name, then! His voice went husky now.

"Touch me, Baby."

I did.

Hot skin, strong, hairy arm, hard chest, hard nipple, harder stomach, all lightly covered in varying thicknesses of the softest, black and silver silky fur, leading down his flat belly — .

I hesitated.

"My Little Girl touches whatever she wants of her big daddy."

I couldn't get my small hand completely around his thick, rigid cock.

"Daddy, your cock feels different than I'd expected."

Hard, thick, and erect, it pulsed in my hand just then and I heard his breath catch a bit.

Daddy's cock in my hand was velvety and weighty, taut skin over a thing alive, not unlike petting Peter, the python, at school—I finally got it, now, Tibby and Tad had named him, for me they'd said.

I stroked down entire the length of my Daddy's long, fat cock and his nads were so vulnerable in my palm, and all musky and damp.

"Baby, smell your palm. Smell me on you."

I did, and giggled, then sniffed again, because I liked it.

"That's the smell of arousal, Baby, what you do to me, and so is this."

"Oh!"

His huge hand slid between my thighs, to finger my stark bright, virgin white lace covered little crotch. My thighs tightened around him of their own accord, as he made me reek pungent musk, too, more than I had when I'd touched myself alone.

I ached, too, now, becoming all breathy, sighey, and clueless about what to do next.

I knew I wanted more, though.

He knew that, too, he always knows me.

Daddy tugged my white lace panties off; sniffing the pussy juice soaked crotch, as his big, tall cock twitched.

I lay there, my naked skin to his hot naked skin, as a vanilla cream pearl grew out of his cock's fat, arrow-like tip. I took my chance, as he watched me gingerly swipe, and taste.

"Mm."

His creamy cum tasted good. Better than vanilla cream.

He was pleased, I could tell, but he didn't smile.

"Open your thighs for me, Baby."

I opened my bare, tan legs wide.

"Bend your knees. Higher." He stared at my naked pussy, for the first time, a wet and needy new pussy, all for him.

He fingered me, ever so gently.

"Oh. Mm." I loved him touching me.

He slipped his long, thick fingers along my slit, parting my soft curls of pubic hair. I loved watching him see me, all naked and all for him. My sex flesh was swollen, sweaty, and musky, as a wild thing in heat.

I wanted, needed him to touch me more.

I lifted my knees higher and wider, without him asking; disgracing my ballet teacher, but opening me, displaying myself to him. "Just like a wanton slut," is what I'd heard an old woman say once, like it was a bad thing.

"That's my good, eager little Valedictorian."

Daddy stared between my thighs, as he slid one of my ankles high over his broad shoulder.

He bent down and kissed me, on my clit! *many* times, and licked, and licked, and sucked on me, until I thought I'd die, over and over again. And something, I don't know what to call it, grew in me.

Can you really, truly die from physical pleasure, like this?!

I wiggled against the desperate feelings running up my spine and twisting round in my belly and below, but he held me fast, sucking on me, on the secret me, tasting me, as I bucked against his face without control.

His tongue flicked here and there, then skewered me, right into me, making my pussy run with tart juice, and teaching me a million new things about my own . . . swollen, begging need, while he slid one long, thick finger inside slippery me.

It hurt at first, as he pushed it in, up to the last knuckle, then moved it in and out, until I stopped hurting, and started wanting more of him.

Two long, thick fingers replaced one and stretched me wider, opening and loosening me, hurting a bit, making me squirm away.

He'd pull me back and I'd try to squirm away again, but my Daddy'd suck on me, and hum, as his fingers did things to me. He hummed the sharp little pains away, nearly making me scream!

When he slipped three fingers inside me, to the final knuckle, I couldn't resist bucking my pelvis hard against him, like my body, my dripping wet pussy had a mad need completely of its own.

"Good, Laila. Fuck Daddy's fingers, Kitten."

I fucked and fucked, I couldn't stand it. I wanted more. I didn't know what it'd feel like, but I wanted it all! I needed him. All of him.

"I need your cock, Daddy. Please? Oh, please? Fuck me, Daddy, please?"

The look in his eyes.

I swear, his cock grew, right before my eyes, as I stared at it, growing as hard as stone, and thicker, and taller than when he'd first undressed, as he wiped his face and lips of my pussy juice, and pulled a lamb membrane condom from the side table and rolled it on.

They're good against pregnancy, but not much else, so know your partner exceedingly well — end of PSA.

Me, I inherited my rubber allergy from Momma.

He lay down beside me, his body radiating heat to mine. He didn't lie on top, like I'd assumed he would, "Missionary position," but pulled my leg over his hard thigh, then rubbed my tender, swollen slit with the side of his thickness, before placing his condom-covered, fat cock tip in my sloppy wet hole, entirely filling its tight, little mouth that was begging for him, yet — .

Stupid me.

I tensed up.

Momma'd be hysterical to see us.

Why'd I think of *her?*

He hugged me closer, his face against mine, his hot breath in my ear.

"Relax, Laila. Open your fresh little cunt to Daddy, like you know you want to, Baby."

He'd never said the "c" word in front of me, the word pierced my ear and mind like a long, fat cock, as now it was *my* cunt he wanted. I relaxed deep inside, and opened my thighs, and my cunt to him.

"Yeah, Kitten, that's it; take all my thick, fat cock inside your tight, sweet little pussy. Damn, you're so tight and wet and—. Oh, fuck."

Daddy drove me mad, talking nasty to me, kissing roughly, his tongue and lips tasting of me!

He had all of me, as he gnawed on my little hard tits, fondled my crazed clit, and pumped inside me, his fat cockhead boring deeper and deeper, pressing hard against the tightness of my virginity, until I held him stuffed deep inside me, his balls pressed against me, his fat cock filling me till it kinda hurt, like I was about to burst, but hurt less as I got used to him.

He'd pull all the way out; before thrusting deep into me, resheathing himself, like he was testing my tight little cunt mouth's new readiness to take him. *All of him.*

He felt like a thick rigid pole impaling me, like a knight's great, hard sword, an *alive*, great invincible sword, in my slick tightness, over and over again, as my pussy juice ran hot in torrents and down my ass crack, like a hungry, salivating mouth, as he repeatedly impaled deep inside me, right into my belly.

He shoved a pillow under my round tan butt, elevating my eager cunt, then mounting on top of me, like a huge, delicious beast, between my thighs, belly to belly, fucking me full out!

My Daddy leaned hard into my tight, slippery pussy, and fucked me so deep!! My cunt making sucking sounds, with every strong, powerful stroke.

Do I call them strokes? I think that's what they're called.

His hairy head was beside mine, breathing hard against mine, his hard thighs forcing mine wider. His ass going up and down like a dog's would mounting his bitch.

I gladly fucked back, without being asked to, until—.

He frightened me.

He was so intense, like a piston or a heat-crazed dog, driving deep into me, over and over and over, yet all distant.

I couldn't see his face; just feel him all over me, against me, inside me. Pissed, I stopped fucking and tried to push him away and wiggle out from under him, but I couldn't, he was so big and I was so little, as he held me fast under his weight.

Finally, he stopped, well, paused, he seemed eager to get back to being a dog piston.

"W-what's wrong, Kitten?"

"I-I could be just any . . . willing cunt." He flinched. "You're not fucking me, Daddy, you're . . . you're . . . ."

I didn't know how to say what I felt, so I pouted like a stubborn, spoiled, stupid baby, while his cock throbbed like scrumptious thick hard iron on fire inside me.

He understood, though, he always understands me.

"Sorry, Laila. Kitten, I didn't mean . . . . I want you, need you so badly, Little Baby."

His pelvis pushed against mine, grinding with a mind of its own into mine. I looked away, trying to stay tough to get what I wanted, and fading. God, he felt good inside me, against me. He sighed.

"Y-you want me to pull out, Baby? To stop?"

"No!! I-I . . . ."

"Don't want to be left out or left behind, while Daddy has his fun? You want to have fun, too, with your big Daddy."

I nodded, pouting still.

"Keep your big brown eyes on your Daddy's, Kitten. I'm not fucking anyone else. There's not another cunt for miles I want like yours. Your Daddy only wants to fuck his sweet, eager Laila's slick, tight, little, oh so 'willing cunt'."

Daddy was making shallow, maddening circles inside me, before grabbing hold of my asscheeks, to thrust deeper into me.

I hadn't really believed that his long, fat thing, his fat cock would fit inside me, now I knew it did, and liked it. I loved it! I was insane for it. For him.

I held tight to him, hugging him tighter and tighter, little apple breasts to broad, hairy chest. Hot breath to hot breath, as he sucked on my tongue, and his cock made me forget all the little girl, good girl crap I'd been taught.

He felt so good inside me, deep between my thighs, bruising them, as he fucked faster in and out of my swollen slickness.

Oh, my God. This is what I wanted. What little school boys couldn't give me.

"I wantta be your whore, Daddy. Fuck me, make me your whore. Please. Please."

His eyes lit up real bright.

"Oh, I will. Guarantee it. That's it, Kitten, fuck Daddy's thick, fat cock; fuck harder, and faster, like the goddamn fuck whore I know you are."

I did what he said and fucked harder, and faster, his thick cock a long, fat, iron poker beating and stoking the center of me into wild, sparkly fire.

SEX IS SOooo PLEASURABLE!!!

A fact hardly to *never* mentioned in class.

Got an A+.

What for, I couldn't tell you now.

Certainly not for experience.

His testicles, nads—*Aren't they fatter, now? They feel fatter, heavier. Is that something else left out of class?*—his fat, swollen hard nads banged against my tight, ass crack, as he hooked my legs higher around his hips, and I slid my palms down his muscled back and dimpling ass, to make him thrust deeper.

Faster.

I don't know how I instinctively knew to do that, except I am my Daddy's "oh so willing little fuck whore" and oh so eager tight cunt.

Long strokes, short thrusts, oh, there was so much, and . . . .

There was this wave.

There can't be a name that truly names it.

This great, fresh energy exploding, like a thousand impossible things inside me; melting my bones, turning me inside out, making me lose all control, all fear; as we both pushed to have all of him inside me, as I made all sorts of shameful whining and moaning sounds I didn't know I could make, before he'd starting banging, pounding, and forging me into something all new.

"That's it, Baby, that's it!"

He held me so tight and whispered into my ear, hot breath burning me.

"I'm cumming, Baby, cumming inside my little Laila's slick, tight litt-."

He shuddered, like great thunder deep inside my belly, until I felt like I was overflowing.

"Ah! Oh, Daddy. MYes. MYes. Ooh."

He thrust again and again, as I felt a rippling pressure deep inside from him and felt myself, my cunt tighten and grasp him, my pussy sucking hard on him, unable to get enough of Daddy and his magnificent cock.

He crushed me to him, crushing my little hard raisin tits against his furry chest, as he ground his crotch against mine; black pubic hair biting through dark auburn; swollen, demanding, and hard flesh grinding into swollen, hot, yielding flesh; all musky, wet, and exhausted with pleasure.

We lay still, his big, fat, long cock still full inside tight little me, perfectly dovetailed together and sealed with his cum and my juices.

His full weight deliciously lying upon me.

We smelled like sex, as his broad, sweaty chest panted hard against my tiny breasts.

"I didn't hurt you, did I, Baby? Did I hurt you much; did I make you too sore, Laila? Did I . . . ? Damn. Damn it, girl."

He was looking up and down us, like he couldn't believe it, all schmooshed together, all hot, sweaty, and musky from grown up play.

Sexy.

"No. You didn't hurt me."

His big hand grabbed my ankle and my Daddy opened my leg to see even more of me, as I looked down, too, and saw him full inside me.

Unbelievable that I could open so wide to straining and nearly burst to take him inside me, yet stay tight enough to—.

My brain turned to mush, as he rewrapped my leg back around him.

I felt so vague and smoky and all kinds of delicious yummy, as I arched against him, to rub my little titties against him.

"I like that, Laila. You sure you're okay?"

"I'm sore, a little. But fuck me, again and again, Daddy. Please? Again and again. And again and again. All night and forever."

I kissed him, like he'd taught me.

His dark eyes became darker and sort of all liquidy moist, as he stroked my loose hair.

He didn't say anything, before I hungrily French-kissed my Daddy, our tongues . . . jousting, parrying and, again, he grew granite hard and thick, deep inside me, inside his new scabbard.

And, we fucked again, and again, late into the school night.

The End.

Neale Sourna's
North Coast Academies' Diary

Yune: Suck My - - - - *[3677 words]*

An Adult Fiction Compiled by

Neale Sourna

Basketball jock Yune gets his stone hard, young Korean American cock sucked by a first time knob munching, K.A. church virgin, while his favorite, bespectacled, brown-skinned teen goddess secretly watches, and then later he's sucked off by a classmate's red-haired, society MILF mom. What a great birthday week he's having!

Fellatio with voyeuristic exhibition, a humiliation cream facial, and a motherly deepthroat, and yes, *gulp*, mom swallows.

ISBN: 0-9741950-7-3
ISSN 1553-8656
Volume 1, Issue 2

July 2006

Yune: Suck My _ _ _ _

by

Neale Sourna

Ah! I *love* havin' my dick sucked. This older bitch really knows what the fuck she's doin'. Not like Amy "The Virgin Clinger," who's got it in her valedictorian seeking head that we're goin' to be together forever.

There's worse.

Her parents *love* me and think me and the Aimster are goin' into twin careers at Microsoft or Google, makin' fat, happy, and brainy Korean American babies. Me and their sweet, forced to go to church daily and double for "Gilmore Girl" Lane's skinny, four-eyed Korean cousin.

That is boring, worships – my – ass – and – the – ground – I – shit – on Amy.

Marry her? Breed with her? Spend all my life to the very gray end with Amy?

No fuckin' way. Not this K.A.

No clichés for me. I'm gonna street board to pussy and riches. The Gravity Games have come right here to nearby Cleveland for the past few years now.

Thanks, Mayor Jane.

Or maybe I'll take my game pro to the NBA. Pro basketball, I can do that. I'm 6'2¾" and still growing, with fast feet, broad shoulders, and a phenom, nearly error-proof free throw.

Or maybe I'll just be sexy in Hollywood; if K.A.'s Rick Yune and John Cho can be handsome, romantic actors kicking James Bond's ass and eating "American Pie," so can I.

I'm a good actor.

My proof? Amy's parents *love* me.

Call me Yune, after the actor, 'cause I look like him, not because it's my real name, which it isn't. Laila nicknamed me. Pretty Laila changes everything and everyone to please herself; think of her as Halle Berry Jr. and THE *hottest* hottie in school.

Understand that Laila ain't got the biggest titties and she ain't no slut, but there's not a guy in class, learnin' or teachin', who's got a dick that loves pussy, who doesn't want to remove those cute gold metal framed glasses and stick her to the balls.

Or the tonsils.

"Oh, fuck! That feels so damn good."

Damn, this PAEB [Parents Education Advisory Board] President can suck some damn crazy hard dick. She's a red haired, red lipstick wearin', ballbreakin' cocksucker.

A classmate's mom.

She's nothin', I mean absolutely nothing like Amy.

I got off with Aims and all, but the quality and power of suck and high level of erotic creativity is not the same.

Not at all.

Plus, Mrs. C swallows.

She should, she's used to that big, fat, long-assed black dick of Mr. C's. How do I know he's packing long, thick, and heavy? The exclusive North Coast country club locker rooms.

But, before I tell you about Mrs. C's swallowing skills, let's keep this in some semblance of time order.

This is how I got forever church virgin Amy to open wide, go down, and gobble my prodigious length of dick.

Milady Laila was at my birthday party, which made it very special, since it is one of the few affairs she's gone to.

Her dad's a total Nazi about that shit. Always afraid she's gonna end up with her little tartan skirt jacked up over her round, tan ass, with one or more of us eager hard dicks jackin' her dark auburn hairy, sweet, virgin's dripping wet pussy.

The Red Hot Chili Peppers' "Suck My Kiss" had just ended and Laila and I'd danced to Dave Matthews, a slow, belly-to-belly dance, so to speak since I'm a foot taller, but the dance was nice and tight.

Amy was not pleased, she normally doesn't get out much, either, but her parents'd definitely let her out of bible class to be at *my* unchaperoned party.

Remember, they think she's my future and that I cannot do any wrong.

Screw that. Amy, she's pretty-ish and nice and all, but I had beautiful, wicked, little Laila and was on a fuckin' cloud.

Laila had to feel my swellin' dick pushin' up against her flat little belly, 'cause I felt her grind up against me. She's a devilish little bitch and knows it, uses it.

Her poor daddy does not—*or maybe does*—know what he's got in his tri-racial baby girl, and keeps her home most nights. What I wouldn't give to have the gold wireframes off and those huge, brown eyes, at crotch level, starin' up at me, with those perfect and pouty, rosy lips wrapped 'round my fat knob.

Or to have her bobbing up and down on my fat, thick stick and moaning that she can't get enough of long, hard me.

Laila had that crazy lithe dancer's bod of hers up against mine, 'til that fucking "Tibby"-"Tyb"-Tybalt the fucking tyrant cuts in.

I wasn't gonna let him and neither was she, but then she glances up at me, all wide eyed, and fucking changes her damn little crazy mind, winks at me and caves to the caveman, who promptly pushed her fine tan ass into a corner for some hard kissin'.

"It's My Party" and all that, but Tyb's about the size and look of a finer boned Vin Diesel.

I'm captain of varsity basketball and taller, and just as broad shouldered, but Tybalt "Tibby" Cross, captain of varsity football and the psycho half of the Cross Twins, has knuckles like hard tempered steel, is a dirty fighter, and truly believes Laila Deever's gonna suck his fat freak some time and give up her virgin's dark auburn pelt to him.

Not if I have anything to say about it.

I'm skinnin' that pristine cunt.

Meanwhile, she's got him eatin' outta her hand. Even if he ain't eatin' no Laila pussy. Him and me both.

Jerkin' us without even touchin' us.

That's Laila.

And Laila pussy. Now, that's a tasty, juicy wet thought a fella can poke around in.

But fuck that, and fuck that little heartless bitch. She'd let him in between us and he'd claimed his trophy, leavin' me "hot and bothered," as Pop calls it. The bitch was playin' us off each other, as usual.

Wanna see the fuckin' pussy-ass ring in my nose?

I stalked out back to Mom's green house, to sulk about losin' Laila from my all too willing arms, and her makin' me eat shit on my fucking day deferring to Tyb fucking Cross.

"Are you all right?

Guess who'd followed me? To console me. Fuck me.

"What'd'*you* want, Amy?"

"What can I do to make you feel better?"

Unreal and shit. I look at her animé cut, straight black hair; knee sock wearing, and forever virgin look.

I start to say, "Fuck off," but say instead, "You can suck this grievous, needy hard-on I got."

Amy's black, almond eyes got big, but fuckin' surprise, she got down on her bare knees right in front of me. Without a serious moment of hesitation.

Personally, I'd thought she'd slap me for sayin' that, or at least run away screamin' to tell mom and dad.

Amy looks real great at that angle, on her knees, mouth at crotch level, all in suburban girl pale pink sweater set and little white pearls.

Oh, yeah, white pearls.

If I'd known Clinger Amy'd kneel and gobble for the mere askin', I'd've asked sooner; especially, since our parents force us to spend so much time together, as study buddies and for Bible reads.

She could've been studying my nads and cock.

In fact, her suckin' my ever in need cock and letting it get thoroughly acquainted with the back of her tight throat could make our peevish nonrelationship more … palatable.

If still unbearable.

Amy's eyes crammed tight when she heard my zipper, but she didn't run. Guess she figured on her own or her crafty mom'd coached her to take one for the team, no matter what I'd ask, and keep me happy.

I'm a rarity around here.

I'm the right pure ethnicity and religion, with rockin' grades, solid popularity, and an assured perfect future, by old line Korean standards. Plus, I'm not hard to look at.

Fuck, I'm Amy's god, she's just not my goddess—Laila is, although it's Amy on her knees about to open wide and worship me.

Plus, I'll have to check if Amy's turning into one of those down the throat or hard cock in the ass virgins, y'know the kind of total slut that'll spread jaw and asscheeks generously wide for a deep whole-in-one, just as long as you don't pop their sweet, so precious virgin's cherry.

What would the cherry police and priests say?

Pokin' everyday could make Amy fuckin' gorgeous.

"Open up, Aims."

She grimaced at the name, she hates having her three letter name butchered, so I do it all the time. She also grimaced to feel the presence of my hot, hardening dick against her soft mouth; presented at crotch level to welcome and receive my gifts.

"Em."

That's the closed mouth sound she made, that kinda disgusted sound girls make between "Mm-Mm Good®" and a full out "Ew." I wasn't forcin' her; I didn't even push down on her shoulder to kneel, so if she wanted out, she could've just gotten up and left.

And said goodbye to ever pleasing her god.

My rosy brown dick was completely hard and looked real good, all huge and fat rubbin' on her wide, flat strawberry pink lips, which I smeared precum all 'round on, before pushin' my fat headed friend into her tight little mouth, forcing her sweet lips to stretch thin to fit me in.

Felt damn good, too; she made a kinda "omp" sound, as my dick-head poked up against her tongue, searchin' 'round and getting' acquainted in its wet and warm new home.

And I'm like, "Watch the teeth, Aims- . . . Shorty."

She liked that. She hates it when I call her Aimster, but "Shorty" is a universal favorite kind of word, so I threw her that friendly bone, 'cause an eager cocksucker' gettin' her teeth out the way is better for my big, fat, happy bone, than a grumpy Aimster with *my bone* to chew.

Ouch.

She smiled as best she could with so much thick, hot meat stretching her wide. I bet her tiny, pink pucker of an asshole's even tighter.

She wasn't my first. No way in H.

I'm captain of the fuckin' championship team and all, but I'm particular about who snacks on me, especially without a balloon. But one thing I'm certain about with Amy, she and a sexually transmitted disease've *never* met.

My "future wife" certainly wasn't the best at lollypoppin'. A first time bone gobbler is almost never great, but like the President's white-haired, mannish mom, Babs Bush once said, a bad blow is better than no blow.

Or somethin' like that.

Generally though, it's always wear a rubber time. My Dad's one of those old guys from the "wild and wooly" sixties, and taught me to ALWAYS carry a swell *(balloon, rubber)*, just in case of coital emergency. Mama wasn't glad about that, but he told her to, well, basically shut up about it, it was man business.

If his son's going to be a first class American male, then . . . .

He has a point.

Think herpes simplex and how many mouths have cold sores, but when herpes gets more and more complex in this complex world; a sick lookin' sore hidin' deep in someone's eager mouth, do you really want that wiped up on your dick?

But Amy's a first timer for everythin' carnal; her parents've kept her locked up tighter than Fort Knox and as ignorant as a gold brick about real sex for as long as I can remember.

Church twice or more a week, and chaperones on our dates.

It's their mistake to let her out this one time.

And I was not complainin'.

By the way, Amy can't stand Laila likin' me so much, and vice versa. Tyb can't stand it either. But I'm not easily intimidated, and her Dad, that big, dark musketeer lookin' fuck — *the sword making master!* — dislikes me a lot less than Tybalt Cross.

I don't know who her daddy's savin' her for, but if either one of us guys gets to poke her, with daddy's blessin', it'll be me.

"Don't stop, Amy."

Novice sluts. They tire easily. Her teeth moved away and her mouth tightened on me, as I pretended Amy was Laila slurpin' on my rod.

It feels so damned good to have a hot maw suck on your peter, even a lame one. Amy hadn't sucked anythin' since her parents broke her off the baby bottle. No sweets; so no lollipops to suck on or ice cream cones to lick for practice.

I gave her a bit of a rest and slid my cock out and 'round her wide, flat lips, flushed cherry red as labia ready and beggin' for pussy penetration.

"Suck the knob, Amy, rub your tongue 'round it, 'long the bottom, too." I moved it in and out her full, soft lips. "Keep your inner mouth firm. Keep it wet."

I pushed deeper into her palate, not too deep, didn't want to choke and scare her, not just. Not before getting' off. I gave instructions for the proper oral handling of a man's hard, hot cock to my brand new cock slut, as she sucked the head rather well.

She is, after all, all used to lots of class and parental coaching.

"Kiss it. Yeah. Harder. Tip to base. Oh, yeah."

Amy was getting' the hang of cocksuckin', but she was startin' to lag a lot. I had to keep her focused on her complicated duties or she'd peter out and I'd have to take a hand to it and finish it myself.

Why finish yourself with two full, sweet virgin lips to suck your balls bone dry?

"Suck my balls."

She grimaced, rather appealingly, actually. Most girls have heard of cocksuckin', but've never considered suckin' fat and musky, hairy ball's from somewhere deep down in your pants. I pushed her head down, gently, but def down.

It's my birthday and she was gonna finish this.

"Kiss 'em. Lick 'em. Suck 'em, Aims. That's the way I like it, girl." I threw her a bone — pun intended, "Laila couldn't do better."

Amy smiled pretty damn big; a smile on lips suckin' your dick makes it all the sweeter.

"You're the best, Amy. Suck me, suck me off, baby."

I'd pushed my fat dick farther into her small mouth and was soft pumpin' it, when I looked up and saw Laila behind Mom's favorite pink rhododendrons watchin'; her big browns behind the wireframes boldly starin', as Amy slurped, kissed, and sucked like a baby on my man milk dispenser.

Sucked like a tired baby; still tryin' to go and go like I wanted, and not knowin' at all when she'd be done workin' this new hard job.

Just so you know, her super protective parents wouldn't sign for her to finish sex health class, back in the day, so I'm pretty certain she's clueless about what happens from the guy's end when you suck and blow on him for this long.

That little pending surprise helped me, and her not knowin' her most detested and beautiful rival watchin' us was addin' to my fun where she was laggin'.

I blew.

Without warnin' Amy, on her sore knees, I blew hard, because I hadn't had a mouth on me in so long and because Laila was watchin' me getting my sperm gun cleaned.

I blew my hot wad into Amy's mouth, while she sputtered all surprised and tried to get out of the way, but I seized her by her black hair and milked and squirted until my last creamy drop hit her golden face.

It was mean, but I got off on it.

So did Laila.

The Aimster was too busy cryin', wipin', and spittin' out cream to curse me.

"Thanks, Aims."

I am polite. And grateful.

Amy got up without making eye contact, without raising her head fully, and ran out, wipin' her face and mouth, like a dog had pissed on her.

I hadn't planned being so rude and bad, but Laila . . . .

Laila was watchin'! She pays attention to bad boys and hard boys, and Tibby is the king of bad and hard at North Coast High, because he is and also to please Laila.

But, I betcha he'd never had Laila stare at his hard, fat dick, and smile broad and sweet, while he blew and smeared hot semen on her rival's face.

* * * *

No. I haven't forgotten the MILF of all MILFs.

I'd delivered some silly PAEB useless crap to her. She's the PAEB President.

She asked how my birthday party'd been.

"Not bad," I said. Got my dick sucked off, while your little neighbor across the way, Ms. Laila, watched, I thought.

Mrs. C smiled, almost like she knew, but how could she?

She said she had a present for me and led me into her husband's den. She is this incredible redhead. (*It's dyed, trust me I'm certain, but that's a later tale about tail.*) She's got this sweet little smirk, all innocent and dangerous simultaneously goin' on.

I mean she's scorchin'.

Think "China Beach" alum Dana Delaney hot. Blam! Blam! Blam! Boobs and hips.

Brains and bodacious everythin' and her sweet hands were all over *me*. She didn't kiss my face or mouth, though. She started on my neck and worked down, with my six pack flat, hairless belly getting' the better brunt of that pleasure, as my dick nearly broke in two snappin' to attention to reach her.

She'd yanked up my letterman pullover and then kissed my belly and unbuckled my pants.

All urgent and shit.

She didn't ask just grabbed, like she was used to gettin' what she wants and she wanted what I had pretty damn bad.

I dumped the sweater, tie, and white dress shirt and let her pull out anythin' I had she wanted.

Our whole class has wet dreamed about her and here I was with my ass against her husband's mahogany desk with *The* Mrs. C, early middle-aged, but hotter than hot, Mrs. C, whose husband advises the school board part-time and runs a big corporation full-time, unzippin' and tuggin' down my hard creased, school dress pants and boxer briefs, yankin' at my springin' to be thick and hard, and all too eager K.A. meat.

Mrs. C went all like "ah" and "ooh" when she pulled out my bat and balls.

I didn't say shit, in case I'd distract her from her appointed goal.

She looked up at me. Pretty Mrs. C on her pale, white knees, in one of the many little black dresses she goes to auxiliary luncheons in.

Her smart ass kids out, her scary, thick husband out, as she looked up at me with that Delaney smirk and softly kissed my dickhead, then swallowed, and swallowed, until her red lips touched, musky black pubes.

"Oh, my . . . ." Damn!

Fucking heaven, her bein' a swallower like that.

I knew I was goin' to, for sure, get to fuck her long, white throat.

She slid off me, draggin' her cupped tongue up firm against me, suckin' hard, until her mouth went "pop."

Mrs. C, without coaxin' or instructions, licked my musky balls and with every darting and lascivious teasing lick, I swear, I felt my cum swell my sacs, especially when she kept lickin' all the way back to that sweet p-spot.

Then, she sucked and massaged each ball with her slick, cock-suckin' red, slender, but highly effective lips; leavin' telltale scarlet marks on me.

Like a fuckin' professional, but free.

Do yah think, like a cheerleader, she's sucked a few before?

And loves it? Like hell yeah and good for me.

She soft bit, then kissed my sacs, then licked up, base to tip and sucked on my dick's head, then another kiss, lick up and suck, over and over. And over and over, while runnin' that mad tongue of hers round and round me.

I grabbed her by her Lady Clairol red hair and rudely pushed my dick to the back of her tight, deep throat.

"Mm," she mumbled, enjoying my selfishness.

That's when I pulled back and jammed my dick in and she took it, every hard thrust, she took it, even looked up at me and nodded her approval, as she grabbed me by my naked ass cheeks and helped me jam my fat dickhead back into her tight, hummin', hot throat, again and again.

Again and again.

My dark balls slappin' against her droolin', white slut's chin.

"Ah!!" I came.

Goddamn, I came and held her fast to my burnin' crotch; no way I don't shoot my hot jiz down *his* whore mom's greedy, red raw, cock-sucking throat.

"Ahh!!!"

I blew hard 'cause the bitch smiled and sucked me in harder, swallowin', and suckin', emptyin' my sacs, like a kid vacuuming out Santa's Christmas bags.

She held onto me, crimson nails diggin' in my ass, suckin' and suckin', until I finally went soft.

Mrs. C didn't spill a drop of me, not a one, as she licked the last drop of hot, pure Yune cream off her swollen, red lip with her sharp, pink tongue.

I didn't think of Laila once, not then, although later, locked in my room, while takin' a hand to my needs, I imagined Mrs. C was Laila, as sweet, wicked Laila made my dick grow thick and hard, then sucked me dry again and again.

And Laila loved it and giggled and licked and suckled me flaccid and begged for more even after I gave her a full Yune hot cream facial.

All in all, not bad, and rewardin' birthday week.

Amy's been distant, though, that's good.

And Ms. Laila's seen my big, fat dick in action, that's *really* good.

But, all in all, no one sucks a long, fat dick dry to the bone like Tybalt Cross' greedy mama.

The End.

Neale Sourna's
North Coast Academies' Diary

Ross: Daddy's Little Whore, uh, Seductress *[8401 words]*

An Adult Fiction Compiled and Edited by
Neale Sourna

Sexy middle-aged stepdad, Ross Deever, wakes naked beside his newly deflowered, multiracial stepdaughter, Laila; then vainly tries abstaining from hitting it again. And again. With a vengeance.

Kitchen table spread, incestuous doggy bang on kitchen floor, and an extensive private lesson in proper *first* cocksucking and throatfucking, a *first* tasty swallow, and her *first* hot cream facial.

ISBN 978-0-9796841-0-4
ISSN 1553-8656
Volume 2, Issue 1

Ross: Daddy's Little Whore, uh, Seductress
by
Neale Sourna

[Part 1 in "Laila: Cozy With Daddy" NCAD Vol 1 #1]

I'd felt touch deprived, and certainly cunt-deprived. I haven't been with anyone in so long. She feels good, damn good, like fucking living, writhing silk; she tastes good, too; damn, she *is* good, and innocent, her dripping wet, teen cunt muscular tight, sucking and milking my lengthy club dry.

The perfect dream night.

The perfect fuck—.

I woke. Early morning dick, fat and hard as granite.

Great dream. Almost.

Disturbing dream.

I sat up, threw the covers back off my nakedness and put my big feet on the floor—on top a used condom; the lambskin membrane [Durex®] kind. She's allergic to latex, so's her mother.

And, there was another "rubber" on top of the trash.

"Fuck."

I absolutely didn't want to look.

Like absolutely not wanting to rip off an adhesive bandage stuck securely to your tender, hairy balls. Rip it off fast or peel excruciatingly slow? I'd usually choose slow, after a long hot soak, but I swiveled 'round, saw her, and leaped off the bed and halfway across the room.

Not a fucking dream. A horny, fucking nightmare!

Not just real "inappropriate" laid over an indiscretion with a stranger, a neighbor, or professional little lady of the evening.

It was Laila, asleep.

Laila, who so resembles a prettier, to my eyes, teen Halle Berry. *My* Laila, in *my* bed. In her mother's and my marriage bed. Naked. Damn delectably naked, with my dried cum smudged on her flat, little tan belly, down into her no longer virgin bush; because of me.

Fuck. I mean, damn. Don't think fuc—!

My God, she's my baby, my one and only daughter. Well, step-daughter, the legal papers of birth and adoption say.

"Damn."

I actually had fucked her. Fucked my Laila.

I'd avoided her, but she'd found me, come to me, and had wanted it, had wanted *me*, and my resistance had flagged fast, as I'd tugged off her brand new, skimpy, white lace hipster panties—*now also lying on the floor beneath my big, sized thirteen foot.*

I'd tugged off her panties and'd put my long, thick tongue in her and tasted her.

And, she'd cum.

I'd pushed open her ballet limber, Tai Chi strong, slim thighs, sucked on her tiny bud of a clit, and licked and tongue fucked her, till her juices had poured down her tight little ass crack, into my greedy mouth, and off my chin.

And, she'd cum.

I'd fingered her, and fingerfucked her.

One long, thick finger. Two. Three. Opening her, widening her musky, pristine virgin passage, until she'd wiggled furiously on my long, thick fingers, and because of them, maddened by them, by me, she'd cried out, begging her daddy, begging *me* to *really* fuck her.

Or had I imagined that?

Imagined that she'd begged for more than tongue and fingers, and I'd given it. That she'd willingly parted her knees higher and wider, inviting me to slide my so eager, fat cockhead and hard, thick shaft into her all the way to my aching, hairy, middle-aged balls.

To fuck her.

And fuck her.

And fuck her.

Until she'd clamped hard upon me and'd quivered all over; so peculiarly similar to when she'd, not so long ago, trembled all over, as a breathless, wide-eyed child on Christmas morning.

Except this was no kid's holiday, and no doll baby I'd given her this time. I'd claimed her sweet cherry and she'd cum, fucked to the hilt on her fath-, on my thick, fat, hungry, and cunt-starved dick.

And damn her cunt, her sweet little puss- . . . her . . . .

She'd tightened around me so hard, as I came. All my lust shot into the nippled tip of the condom, buried deep in Laila's slick, wet, first heat, and I came.

I came deep inside my gold wireframe wearing, little private schoolgir—.

"Damn."

Her mama's gonna fucking kill me. But, that ever selfish bitch would have to come home for once to do that.

I went to the bathroom and looked.

Turned on the glaring light and took a damn good look in the mirror at Ross Deever; old enough to have a daughter soon to be in college. Mature enough to have silver hair speckled in the black on my head, my chin, and body, all of which was still fit; hard enough, strong enough, and handsome enough to turn heads of schoolgirls and their mothers both.

Laila says I look like a "dangerous musketeer or a debonair cavalier," or some such dashing, literary bullshit, as—.

"What the . . . ?"

It was tickling my lip, entangled among the black of my well-lined goatee and mustache. I spat at it, it wouldn't dislodge, and so I pulled it out.

"Fucking damn."

It was deepest dark auburn. My Laila's hair is shoulder-length, *medium* dark auburn, on her head; *deepest* dark auburn is the color of her beautiful, silken hairs on her pretty little wet pussy, which I could still feel, smell, and taste.

"Fuck me."

I took showers; multiple, hot and cold.

To wash away my sins. To deaden my growing urge and memory of her lithe, bare flesh against my hard, hairy body; her smooth, poreless bronze, multiracial skin sharply contrasted against the age and single hue of mine, while she'd made my cock burn, while just lying beside me, afterwards, smiling in her sleep—contented.

After I'd fucked the hell out of her half the night.

I'd been avoiding her last night, had taken a long, cold shower, and was still avoiding her afterward, with all the strength I could muster, yet *she'd come* to me, her mind made up to have me; she'd shed her fuzzy, old, pink chenille robe with the happy teddy bear on the bottom, to show the delicate, white lace panties and bra she'd bought without me knowing, to wear just for me.

For me!

Laila'd kissed me, like a desirous, knowing woman, not a doting, innocent daughter, but I'd resisted, until she'd stripped off the pushup bra, revealing her perfect, apple round, golden brown breasts with tasty hard raisin nipples, still puffy with her youth; and she'd kissed me again.

It was *her decision* to take the plunge. She's of age to consent and I think I . . . .

Yes, I-I did remember asking if she were certain.

And when I was . . . when *we* were completely done, the first time, she'd asked, had begged for more.

For more of *me*, and *my cock*.

For me to slide and stuff my fat, long cock back into her and fuck her sloppy wet, tight pussy even more.

I'd been "gentle," at least, been careful; hadn't drawn any blood, didn't rip or tear her, had coaxed her, so tiny-to-me, 5'2¾", 104 pound body and courted pure, distilled desire from her, from my little girl's magnificent, budding woman's body; the same tiny body that I'd escorted new into this world.

The first man ever to hold this amazing child in my enormous hands.

It's maddening.

Laila was always a precocious kid. Then, last night!

She'd wanted *me*, needed *me*, and not that fucking little bastard across the street. Laila'd eagerly opened wide to me, like a flower bud, and blooming brightly; like an ember, she'd flamed, and enflamed me, consumed me.

Making me mentally "wax poetic" which is wholly unlike me.

She'd wiggled, oh so deliciously, against and on my fingers after I'd massaged her panty covered crotch till her juice soaked through, before I'd pulled her white lace panties down her tan thighs and off, to finger her hairy, swollen, and slick cunt.

I shouldn't call it . . . call her that.

But, I'd called her *that* and more, in my heated lust, and she'd loved that, too. Words like "pussy." And she'd begged me to call her those names. "Cunt." "Whore." Words not allowed in this house with an innocent, private school-aged girl in it.

My slick pussy. My tight, wet cunt. My wanton little whore.

"Damn. Damn. Damn!"

This morning's showers, hot to scald clean, cold to dampen my eagerness to lust, weren't working.

My sweet, little girl lay asleep in my bed, naked, brown skinned— *beautiful, multi-race skin of red and white and black*—mixed to tan perfection. Huge, intelligent brown eyes; myopic, root beer brown. Shoulder-length, thick, wavy, dark medium auburn hair, and loosely curled pubes of deeper color, so silken, and . . . .

I was working my cock, long before fully realizing it, and when I did I couldn't let go of stroking and stroking the length of my swollen dick, remembering her presenting her sweet girl breasts so eagerly and opening her ballet schooled legs wide and trusting, to present her ever so fuckable, untouched, and wet virgin's cunt.

The one I know every boy in her school wants, and half the educational administration's men as well.

I know I've seen their eyes. That's why I've always been so protective of her, but now . . . .

The head of my cock still remembered the first touch of her, the give of her opening to me, and my throbbing balls that banged up hard against her all now know Laila's taut and taboo cock sheath intimately, biblically; mine, fully claimed, more than once.

I stroked my dick harder this time, just as I'd done so recently, when I'd known Laila was watching me, from her cousin Taffy's window. Watching me as I'd thought of her and pulled my cock till my cream had jetted across, onto the steaming bubbling water of the hot tub.

As I did again now.

"Laila, you cunt, you fucking tight, little sopping wet cunt, you eager little whor — ."

She'd rubbed her finger across my dick tip last night, without me asking, then she'd sucked my cream off her dainty, little finger; the same one she'd sucked in her baby dreams.

Laila'd tasted my precum, and loved it, before begging me; not her want to be boyfriend Yune or that fucking, thick neck Tybalt Cross next door, she'd begged *me* to fuck her "again and forever."

My cum came hard now, splashing hot onto the shower walls and floor, as the water tried washing my stubborn suds down the drain.

When I was breathing normal again, the blood recirculating to my stupid brain, I realized she'd wake soon and . . . .

What would I say to her?!

What would she . . . ?

She could have me arrested. Couldn't she? I should have me arrested.

Who'd call and tell her mother, the missing woman? And if she'd been here like she's supposed to, taking care of her wifely duties, my starving cock's needs, Laila and I'd never . . . .

At least I believe Laila and I'd never . . . .

I glanced at the time.

We'd be late. We're never late. She'd be tardy and the headmaster'll ask her:

"Why're you late, Ms. Deever?"

"Well, I slept naked with my father, after he popped my cherry and then we'd fucked, crazy hard all night and . . . ."

If I just wake her quickly and rush her, we shouldn't have time to talk. Not and get to the Academy on time.

I slipped on a robe, quietly cleaned up my bedroom of "evidence," and woke her. I harried her to get ready. She rubbed her sleepy eyes, with that baby pout of hers beneath the disgruntled little frown.

Same as every morning. Except being in my bed.

Yes, a normal morning.

Until I saw her sit up and her naked breasts, the size of Golden Delicious apples, settled into place. Fuck me. She stretched and they resettled once more.

Y'know, I've noticed lately that her cup size is fuller. Should a father, step or blood, notice that kind of thing? Is it bad of me to notice? Damn, she moved and they moved again, pointed actually.

My damn cock was noticing, too.

I also noticed again, with an unbelievable feeling of self-satisfaction on my stupid part, that generous splatter of my dried cum spread across her tan, young belly and down deep into her dark auburn pubes.

My fucking stupid, incestuous ass is going to the deepest, hottest Hell.

She grabbed her teddy bear robe off the bed where I'd just lain it and she went straight to her room, seemingly unmindful that she was naked beneath and had been fully so, in my bed.

Or that I'd ruthlessly and thoroughly fucked and cored her bow-legged, for half the night.

She bathed and dressed, as normal, while I couldn't deal with making breakfast. Not normal. I told her we'd be "crazy late," as she would say. I told her we'd stop at the fast food drive thru, just this once, and then straight to class.

"Come on, Laila! School. Now."

I'll have to deal with it after school, but not now. She stopped dead in her tracks.

"W-What's the matter?"

Maybe I'd hurt her. She's solid, but so tiny; I'm huge beside her. I'd fucked her pretty damn hard; and more than once, in my licentious, incestuous greed.

Deflowered, in her safe home by someone she trusts with all her soul.

Her first time with anyone, having her sweet cherry skewered, riding on *my* fat dick. Not Tyb Cross'. Not Yune's. My daughter's first fuck, riding *my* long, fat, and ruthless cock.

Focus, man.

She was at the door, still standing there, in red, white, and blue, in her solid dark blue blazer over white shirt, old school, man tie, with her herringbone, pleated skirt, staring back at me through her fragile little, white gold wireframes.

"Daddy, what time is it?" I checked my watch.

"Late. We gotta go." She sighed and shook her head in exasperation; y'know, in that way girls always do with errant fathers.

"It's Saturday."

Damn. Fucking damn.

She was right.

She rolled her large brown eyes behind the lenses, dropped her heavy book bag, and then scuffed her heels on the polished wood floor and stairs all the way, as she dragged back upstairs to bed.

To *her* bed not mine. Thank god.

Alice crossed my mind then; her best friend and normal partner in crime. What would she tell Alice? Who would Alice tell?

Fuck that. Can't think of that, not now.

If I cleaned my incriminating bed sheets and pretended, do you think she'd believe it was just a dream? She has extremely vivid dreams all the time, confusing things she's said in them to me with reality in which she hasn't spoken to me yet.

Would she truly believe it was a hyper vivid dream, if I pushed the theory?

Hopefully, the physical proof wasn't as bad as I thought, that her little pussy wasn't too cock sore from me being so big and stretching her, riding her for her first time, let alone before I'd heartlessly banged her relentlessly again, like she was a damn fucking street whore, whose cunt I'd bought for the night.

Vivid dreams. Yeah, stick to that.

She might fall for it, despite her being incredibly not stupid, and despite her mind being incredibly sharper, with a memory usually better than mine.

Lie. Yeah, lie.

An utterly, desperately stupid plan, but worth a try.

* * * *

I was working in my studio, until — .

"Daddy, you made my little pussy so deliciously sore."

Laila's voice was a distracting, disconcerting warm purr in my ear, as she kissed my neck, her arms draped around my shoulders, her wireframes against my skin, and her apple breasts against my broad back.

I'd been drafting — *or at least at my drafting design board* — doing very little all day.

My studio and forge are behind and attached to the house, with the residence facing one street and the business a private mews.

She'd snuck up behind me, in my dazed distraction, and she'd stepped up on the chair's foot rail, and slipped her arms tightly around me.

Her arms around me isn't unusual.

Kissing me isn't, either.

But the purring, like that, in my ear, making my balls ache with those words, was . . . unusual. I'd washed the bed linen, hidden her pushup bra and lace hipster panties, still smelling of her and crinkly with her dried, sweet pussy juice, and I'd garbage bagged the used condoms.

An entirely in vain, comic activity, while I'd been seriously endeavoring a false pretense. Yet, it always seems somehow to work in novels, sitcoms, and soap operas.

I, unfortunately, never could boldface lie to her, especially if the lie wasn't to outright protect her. Now, lie to her mother; yes, that I can do, like a breeze, but to Valedictorian frontrunner Laila, the darling owner of my heart, and now growing stone hard cock, no.

"W-Watch your language, Laila."

She chuckled, kind of nasty and deep in her throat, right in my ear, not a girlish giggle, or nervous one. A sexy one.

That sound went straight through my ear drum to my balls, making them tighten and sweat.

Damn.

We'd broken more than one barrier last night; her virginity, her innocence, our long-standing clean language taboo. And the most important: parent and child.

Irreparably shattered.

Unfucking unforgivable.

Unfucking unforgettable.

"Get off me, Laila. I'm you're father not one of your wannabe boyfriends."

"Hm. Really?"

She slipped her hand into my open shirt neck to touch bare, hairy chest and scratch at my nipple, which hardened up so tight under her greedy little fingertips and short, polish-free nails, that I felt it like an alarm going off, all the way down to my scrotum, and that alarm went up and up, *many* decibels inside me, when she kissed me a second time, on my neck, which unraveled me.

And, she also included a little cock-stirring bite of my ear, that took my breath away.

"L-Laila, please."

The wrong thing to say, said in the wrong way, as I closed my eyes, realizing I should at least act outraged, and not plead, but I liked her small hands on me, her thick, soft, wavy hair against my skin, I loved her boldness.

She'd always been a bold and affectionate little girl and she'd proven a bold, enthusiastic, if gladly inexperienced, quick learning lover.

Thank god no one, not basketball captain Yune, and certainly not her football captain "Tibby" had ever had her, before me.

Not that I should. Not that I'd planned to, but . . . .

Damn. *Damn.* Get a backbone, man.

"Stop it, Laila."

"'Stop' what?"

I pushed her arms away, knocking things off my design table, and nearly fell on my face getting out of my chair and away from her.

From the one person I love most.

The one person who could always hold her own in conversation since she'd been knee high to me.

The person who had an amused and all too grown up smirk on her sweet, berry colored, full lips; so perfect for a man's cock.

Shut up crazy thoughts!

"Oh. So, Daddy, you're going to ignore what *we* did? All of what *you* did to me? Repeatedly. And, oh, so enthusiasticall—."

"Stop it. That was a mis—."

"A 'mistake'? How many times? And *you made love to me*, Daddy, like I asked, not just fucked me, you made *love* to me. Over and over again. Got off in me. Over and over again."

I opened my mouth, but nothing sensible or audible came out. She, however, was loquacious and informative, as she swiveled in my still warm, just vacated task chair.

"Y'know, the other girls, Alice too, they've told me what their first times were like. Pain. Blood. No orgasm. Boring. Not fun at all actually.

"You were wonderful, Daddy! You made mine simply a wonder! I came every time—*when you fucked me and when you ate me out, too.* Oh, it was *so fantastic,* cumming with that impossibly chunky hard cock of yours all stuffed and jammed up into me, all screwed up tight inside me, filling me like—."

"STOP THAT!"

My head.

The one on my shoulders was about to explode, from everything she was saying and how she was saying it; and she wore over her apple-round, firm breasts a snug, peach colored tee, beneath which her naked, braless little nipples poked in reaction to my voice, hardening to hard raisins.

Distracting, tasty raisins on sweet golden apples.

I just barely forced my gaze away from them.

"Go to your room."

"Why?"

"You don't question me, just . . . just go."

"Not to *your* room?"

"Laila!"

Her nostrils flared, as she squinted at me, thwarted and peeved.

I'd probably pay for it, as she flounced out and I watched her finely shaped tan legs and that fine, round mount of ass of hers working the hell out of the matching peach colored short shorts she was wearing, on this unseasonably warm, non-school day.

No panties.

She *always* wears panties. Goddamn it. Why wasn't she wearing panties? Why was her beautiful ass *jiggling* like that?

Why the Hell was I noticing?

I didn't follow her, to console her, to beg her forgiveness, or any such insanely stupid thing. I was afraid to pursue her, a little girl, who barely comes up to my pits.

I worked instead.

I design and make custom weapons; bows, crossbows, and swords, especially, are my specialty, for theater, film, fairs, martial artists, and collectors. But my drawings today of new, deadly swords looked more like steel phalluses with scrotum hilts.

So, I put down my pencils and pens and got physical.

I set the fire on high and heated metal in my forge and then sweated and pounded metal, and I became more focused, as I edged and polished the most recent blade I'd made for Laila.

My best designs for her have always been great sellers, especially since the fighting TV femmes "Xena: Warrior Princess" and "Buffy: The Vampire Slayer" began wielding.

I always modify the Laila designs slightly, so she has the one and only original. I've been offered outrageous sums and other substantial bribes, more physical and too strange to repeat, for an original, unmodified Laila design.

Collectors've even gotten ugly about it.

Fuck 'em.

I do the special designs for my Laila, and for no one else.

This new blade was incredibly sweet, too. Perfect. Balanced. Elegant. Slim yet shapely, and strong. Deadly. A smart blade. A beautiful blade. Just like Laila.

I couraged up and, feeling the heat of the shop leaving the sweaty skin on my bare chest and back, I went inside with her new blade.

Laila wasn't in her room.

Or in the house.

Fuck it. I had a damn good idea where she was and went out across the street. The Crosses could afford a more expensive home, but the wife and kids love this neighborhood. And like ours, theirs is a "mixed race" family, but Alida Cross and her fraternal twin sons, wry Tad and brusque Tyb, always seem to be in my way.

Vin Diesel Jr, Tybalt, most especially.

I, insistently, rapped on the window.

"Tibby" was on the sofa passionately, deeply kissing my daughter, his tongue at its busiest, as his big fingers were working their way into her shorts. I rapped harder, about to break glass. He looked up, lax, until seeing me shirtless and sweaty with a shiny, real sword on my shoulder.

His eyes bucked wide, Laila's did not, not even after she put on her glasses.

The petite bitch had expected me.

I've seen her manipulate others; she's usually not like that with me, at least not so blatantly. She knows I hate this Cross boy; he thinks he owns her, which of course he doesn't, but she plays him off me and me off him, when she's mad at either of us.

Told yah, she'd make me pay.

Alida opened the door, looked at me, then at the sword. It was still in its scroll worked scabbard.

"Laila, dear, I believe your father wants you home. Now."

Laila came out, without a moment of hesitation, but a lot of peeved silence, as she passed me by and Alida called after us.

"Remember, Ross, they're young. They have to find out sometime. Better at home, under our supervision, than in the wild and nasty streets. Really Ross, sometimes, you really need to watch where you unsheathe and bury that hard blade of yours."

I looked back, and stumbled, momentarily thinking Alida knew about last night, before realizing she'd just wanted a reaction out of me, a second look back from me.

Perhaps she had a point.

If I were going to drop my pants and fuck wet and willing pussy, why hadn't I called Alida? A woman my age. She'd open wide for me in an instant, and had, once, before when I'd . . . .

I went inside, locked the door and shut our drapes. If the world isn't intruding into my business with its false concerns, with "Have you heard from your wife, Carline, lately?" it's tempting my baby out from under my direct protection.

The babe in question was waiting, arms crossed, narrow hips well-placed over tiny feet, set to do battle, so I spoke first.

"This is yours."

I tossed the safely sheathed blade to her and she caught it grace-fully, then, sensuously—*or at least it peculiarly seemed so to me*—she slid the blade out of its scabbard, to scrutinize my work before glanc-ing at me; more, I think, to make certain my gaze was full on her.

It was.

She wielded the blade one handed with the scabbard in the other, as an additional warding off shield.

As I'd taught her. Beautiful moves. Strong. Thoughtful, yet intui-tive. Elegant. Passionate.

I swallowed hard, hoping the abrasive lump choked behind my Adam's apple, like a twenty pound rock, would find its way down to block whatever chief source of betraying blood was attempting to thicken, harden, and hoist my dick.

I needed distance. From her.

Heading directly past her to the kitchen was a plan, until she blocked my way with the unsheathed blade across my bare chest.

Flat, blunt side against me, but she could slice me badly, up or down, if she so desired. Laila slid the cool metal across my nipples, before stepping around and turning the deadly weapon, to lightly drag the sharp blade's pointed tip down my belly.

It made a faint sound while coursing through my chest hair. The blade traveled in and out of my navel, and down that hirsute glory path, below a man's waist, on the trail to his . . . .

The pocket-sized bitch was getting to me, and knew it. I swear, sometimes, she's too often her mother's child.

"That's enough, Laila. Put it away."

"But I love my rigid, new blade; he's perfect for me and fits, if a tad fat and snugly, sliding in and out my barely broken in, wet-oiled scabbard, which—."

"Don't. Say. Another. Damn. Word. This isn't one of your English contest fictions for college, this is *our lives*. Put it away. Wash your hands and face of 'Tibby,' and wash your smart, little mouth out, as well, then come to lunch. Or do you not understand me, young lady?"

Again the squint and flounce to her room. Damn that girl's jiggling backside. And why hadn't I said in confident boldness that there will be absolutely no repeat or continuation of last night's antics?

Why hadn't I?

* * * *

Lunch was intense, silent, and sulky. I'd made lunch so Laila was doing the dishes.

Maybe I should've done them myself and sent her to her room. She was at the kitchen sink, knowing I was watching her, and trying not to, or more specifically trying not to think about what we'd done before, last night, when she'd come to me, and asked me, and I'd—.

Never watch a woman or girl you want for too long, especially one you've already been blessed to have once, or twice.

Or more.

I told myself, convinced myself that I was truly going to apologize to her, or offer some stupid token of failed fatherly duty.

Who am I fucking kidding?

I remembered her smell, her taste, the way she felt—*her bold eagerness to be taken by me*—and I needed to feel her against me, now, as I stood over her and she leaned back, until she was against me.

She dried her hands, then took my big hands in her tiny ones and placed them over her petite, pert breasts. My hands eagerly found their way under her shirt, which she slowly pulled up over her little tits, so I could see her pert little titties in my large, hardened palms, as I tweaked them, played with them, and heard her breathing change.

Laila was undoing her shorts.

"I'll get that, baby."

My hand seemed enormous, as it slid down her brown belly, deep into her peachy short shorts, and she moaned, as the musky heat rising out of her pubes made my mouth water, and my balls ache. There wasn't room really for all that was in those tight, little shorts, as I stroked and fingered her, as she held my big hand down between her thighs.

"Don't stop, Daddy."

Not happening, as I whispered hot, obscene things in her innocent ear, kissing her neck, nibbling her tiny earlobe.

Whether I led her or she led me over to the table, I no longer recall.

I do recall her willing eagerness in pushing down her shorts without panties beneath, now musky and soaked with her anticipation's wet lust. I stared at her wild, untrimmed garden.

My pants dropped, too, and my fingers slid through her profusely slick valley. I sucked on her tongue and pert breasts, I dimly recalled that this was how I'd gotten into trouble the previous night, hard riding, fuzzy balls deep in fresh, young, untrained cunt, between the smooth, young thighs of my own daughter, stepdaughter.

The "step" part makes a difference, doesn't it?

I vaguely recalled all that, but right now didn't care, especially since she didn't, as I repositioned her on the table to dick her, but as soon as my fat cockhead touched her sweet, slick and swollen hot flesh—.

I somehow half came to my senses and sensibility.

"No. Wait. We—."

"In my shorts."

"What?"

"My shorts. In my short shorts, Daddy. Please hurry."

I was a lot confused and just picked them off the linoleum and handed them over to her. What the . . . ?

A hidden pocket. A condom.

Hm, well, how long had that been there? In my little virgin schoolgirl's pocket, hidden from me? And for whom had it been there?

For me?

Or for Tibby?

Or her "gold-skinned Korean" young Yune, even?

The questions left my mind, as she opened the foil and dressed me; like a banana in bio, huhn?

Damn, the pleasant touch of her little hands possessing me, stroking me. I selfishly thought that I'll have to teach her how to use those smart and small hands to whack me off the way I like. It's a useful skill for a girl, in the open in a car, under a restaurant table or a lap blanket beneath a tree at the distributor's picnic.

Laila's mother, Carline, has fearsome skills in all; hands, pussy, jaw, and ass.

And here I was fucking Carline's baby, the one she'd sworn wasn't mine and yet had married me to protect and teach.

Yeah, I was teaching her.

I fucked my Laila, again, slid my condom sheathed fat cockhead into my pretty baby's tight, sweet, wet, and oh so willing pussy. Just fit me like a perfect new glove trimmed in deep darkest auburn hair, any tighter and I wouldn't've fit.

Most perfect. Delicious. Damn. Goddamn.

She sighed nicely.

I fucked her, facing her, kissing her, watching her react to me, watching her little titties under her pulled up shirt. Her titties jumped and jiggled at every move, as she pulled her knees high and wide and saw and felt what I did to her, filled her; nearly letting her cum, then making her wait, as I fucked her, controlled and directed her wanton, young lust—giving her my full parental guidance in her sexual education.

My thick, experienced cock slipping in and out of her petite, fresh, and so damn juicy cunt.

Both of us laughing for the joy of being together like this, as she dropped a shoe to put a tiny bare foot on my black and grizzle haired chest, before I kissed that foot and sucked it 'til I stirred my dick in her and hit something special in her—Laila gasped then moaned, her toes popped out my hot mouth, and her cunt sucked hard on me.

Sweet, like hot apple pie.

I picked her up and put her on the floor where I kept fucking her, as I turned her this way and that, to find that right, extra special position.

Ah.

"Doggy style, Laila. Just right for a randy little bitch in heat like you."

Rough, black Rottweiler mounting petite, dark red Spaniel, and the Spaniel begged.

"Oh, Daddy, don't stop. Fuck me. Oh, fuck me."

Her voice was sweet, low, and pleading, as I fucked her.

It was a perfect position, fucking like dogs, like animals in the fucking wild, easy to hit the right spots inside her, yet core her deep. I had her good. Every time I fucked back into her, she'd say a little "uh."

"Uh, uh, uh, uh."

Laila's fascinated with words and meanings, loves her words, loves to talk, to manipulate with her words; she couldn't talk now, she was too fucking close to her heat's edge.

I shoved her head down by the neck, like you do a horny bitch in an alleyway, tilting her so I sank deeper into her.

She spoke. Sort of.

"Uh. Ooh. Yesss."

Goddamn, I was making her whine.

She dutifully held her head down, medium dark auburn hair all about, resting on her elbows and forearms, as I held her sopping wet cunt high, holding her tight by the thighs, like a wheel barrel, splitting her with my big body, and still Laila wiggled her narrow, girl's hips 'round in delicious, pleasure-seeking circles, fucking me, as I fucked her.

Her tight pussy looking like it was about to be pulled inside out, as I pulled out and seeming about to burst, as I forced all my great size deep into her need and want, forcing the cunt juice to foam and drip out of her.

Her pleading and wiggling . . . .

I didn't bother fighting the urge to pound, and grind her tender sex to all Hell, as a favorite song's lyric went through my head, Nine Inch Nails' "I Want to Fuck You Like an Animal.©"

Damn. Fucking. Straight.

Little Laila wrapped her legs back around me, so I let go, leaned forward, palms on the floor either side of her and kept at it, fucking her, grinding my fat balls up hard against her, against her clit, my cock swelled to its fullest, stretching her dripping wet, little pussy ring to her limit, as I felt my cockhead sink into her up to her belly.

Fuck, all the way up to her heart.

"I'm cumming, baby, and I can't stop." Goddamn. "Ah!!!"

How I came! And came hard, and long! Her mother'd never gotten me off better.

"Daddy, don't stop, please, don't stop, now."

I did as she begged me, I continued fucking Laila, my little Laila, until she, too, came in cock grasping spasms, as I continued fucking her this way and that through it all, through her entire cumming.

Cumming of age, huh?

If you've never done that, fucked her through her cumming, you *really* should. *Your* tight, little cunt'll love it, too.

"Oooh, Dad- . . . ."

Our naked bodies against each other; sweat and heat lubricating us; cock in pussy, perfect fit, reeking of hot, wet, fresh, and musky sex.

Nasty sex.

Illegal and immoral, too, right?

When I finally pulled out from her, I took a quick peek at her from behind and saw a river of cunt juice pour out and how raw she was. I tested her and poked back at her with my fat cockhead.

"Ow!"

I'd used her badly and she hadn't complained, had taken it, every inch, every centimeter of, not a boy's cock, but a full grown man's needy cock, hard, fat, and long.

"When can we fuck again, Daddy?"

"My, my. My greedy little cunt wants more of her Daddy's cock, so soon? Her Daddy's big, fat, long cunt-busting cock?"

"Mm-hm."

"No more cock for you tonight."

She turned over to pout.

"Oh. But—."

"No 'but'." There was a pun in there, but I let it pass. "Go up and run a bath, hot. An Epsom salt bath'll do your soreness good. Remember, you have to take good care of your equipment—."

" 'Especially when you've used it roughly.' I remember. Is your equipment sore, too?"

"No, not exactly. At least not like yours."

" 'Exactly,' what then?" Some people calm down after sex, some get sleepy. Some, like my little girl, get hyper. Then again a good, hard fuck on the kitchen floor can make just about anyon . . . .

"Bath. Now."

"I don't wantta take a bath, I—."

"Will do as I say." Pretty pout, again. Wait for it. "I'll join you."

Her bright eyes lit up behind the wireframes.

"You will? You'll get in with me?"

And that smile of hers, I could do things with that smile and that pretty, fresh berry shaded mouth with the perfect pearl teeth.

* * * *

"Make love to me, Daddy."

"Behave yourself."

We'd been in the tub, soaking; she was lying back against me.

"Hm. I saw Yune's cock, at his birthday party."

I didn't answer. I was a little afraid to, and remained silent. So, of course, she continued, to get a rise out of me.

"Yune's long, hard, fat dick, Am-. . . *someone* was sucking it. Not very well. But he came, knowing I was watching him. He came in her mouth. On her face. *She* hated that."

She giggled, and'd left out the name, but I knew she knew the girl, and didn't like her much, at least not when it came to Yune in the middle. That was a small circle of intrigue, I know who my little girl knows or they're off her list of acquaintances.

Sucking that fucking Yune.

I knew I shouldn't've let her go to his party, and someone shouldn't have let Amy go either, poor girl, poor stupid little girl trying to impress a boy who doesn't want her.

"I wonder what Yune tastes like," my little naked girl said.

"None of your damn business what he tastes like."

She abruptly swung around in the water, in the hyper enthusiasm teens nearly always seem to have. Her eyes looked extra dark without eyeglass lenses.

"Daddy, I love your taste so much. Teach me how to suck your dick and drink your cum."

Where'd she learn to construct a sentence like that? At least she was asking me and not Yune or Tibby.

I still don't believe that I didn't say anything nor react, but I know how to get a rise out of her, too. She pouted a little before licking my nipple, but the Epsom salt's bitter taste made her face pucker up like a Scrunchy™.

I'm afraid I laughed, and got out.

"Daddy, it's not funny! It's —."

Laila can read just about anyone and she's damn near psychic with me. My expression'd changed when the thought finally fully

registered with me, and she realized she was getting what she wanted—her first lesson in sucking her father's fat dick.

There will be swallowing, of cum as well as cock. I require it when I am so serviced.

"Eager for your next lesson in being Daddy's eager little whore?"

"Yes."

Such seductive bright eyes and sultry voice, when'd she get those?

I turned on the shower and rinsed us both off; I didn't want her tasting bitter salts. We dried off, massaged, and oiled up with edible coconut oil, as I whispered in her ear things she was going to do for her Daddy, before pushing her down, still completely naked, on the floor beside my bed, between my knees for her next Sex With Daddy Lesson.

"I'm not your little boyfriend, Yune; I'm bigger and more demanding. It's harder than you think. Or so I hear.

"And I won't let you stop once you start. There'll be no pouting or attitude to get your way out. I've spoiled you, pretty baby, and you're going to spoil me tonight.

"So, if you want to do this, you'll do it right, and to the finish. Still want—?"

"Oh, yes."

What man doesn't love naïve eagerness in an innocent beauty on her knees about to say, "Ah," before her first throat full of you? I sat and pulled her by the dark red hair to my crotch, smashed her pretty face against my equipment to let her feel it up close and in her face, before I rubbed my cock on her lips to take it.

Just like she'd said Yune did to his little cocksucker. Poor Amy, Yune got off on her and so had my naughty little Laila, by proxy.

Now, Laila was *my* Amy.

She eagerly took me in her mouth, barely. It apparently started to register on her, as I hardened and swelled, filling her jaws, just how big I really am and how, well, I've a lot of fat meat for such a pretty little mouth.

I let her slide back off, as her mouth and my dick slowly got acquainted.

She licked around her lips to lube them then licked my pisshole, and it felt great. She stretched her pretty mouth over me and sucked my knob, and it felt great.

She slid back off and slid her teeth flat along my shaft, before taking me in again.

"Fucking damn. Laila?"

"Hm?"

Her questioning innocent face was upturned to me, with my fat dick in her small mouth, stretched to the limit all around me.

"Where'd you learn to do that? To use your teeth like that?"

She pulled my cock out of her mouth with a nice little pop.

"No where. Thought it might feel good to you. Was I wrong, Daddy?"

"No. Do it again, then Daddy's gonna teach you how to swallow his sword to the hilt."

I stood up, I like it standing. She did her teeth trick again for a bit and then I gave her more instructions in being her Daddy's Whore.

"Relax your throat, baby, like you do for church choir and girl's glee club. That's it. Damn, what a fine, eager slut you are, take it all, baby girl."

She was taking an admirable amount of my length down her throat, as I filled her.

She choked, looking a bit scared.

I pulled out and let her relax, as I stroked her face and hair, but didn't let her pull away.

"Daddy's bigger than you thought, isn't he?" She nodded, but eventually licked her lips and opened wide again. "Good girl."

She relaxed her throat better, as I pushed my thickness in.

"Look up at me, look up while you swallow me."

She valiantly tried to see my face, until her flushed lips were pushed all the way into my pubes. I felt her hot breath on me and her lips top and bottom and my cock full down her tight, virgin throat.

Cherry number 2 taken.

An overachiever like her loves praise, so I praised my sweet, little darling.

"Laila, the cocksucker. *My* cock sucker. Daddy's sweet little, Val-e-*dick*-torian, cocksucking whore."

I slowly fucked her throat and she took it, but tired quickly. I bucked it up and pulled most the way out to let her rest.

"I'm gonna fuck your little mouth, baby girl, until I cum, no let up. Understand? Play with your little titties, baby. Daddy wants to see you play with your titties, before I fuck my baby's sweet, little mouth, and cum all in you."

I watched her play with her tits, while my cock lay in her warm mouth, her tongue sucking up against me and questing with its tip, before I pushed and she took it.

I shallow fucked her mouth a few, letting her get used to me, and then I fucked all the way down her snug, wet and hot throat.

Out.

Then back in.

My sweet, little whore of the full throat fuck, on her first time.

I saw her fingering her wet pussy, but mostly I loved the way she sounded.

"Uhn-uhn-uhn . . . " was all she could say, as I fucked her tight, little greedy gullet.

She'd be hoarse; raw, sore throat deep on both ends Monday for class.

My balls drew up, and I mercilessly gave no warning this time, letting the first generous burning volley hit the back of her red-flushed throat and battered, fleshy tongue.

I always have plenty of cum with a whore I want as much as her, and it comes out of me like a bullet from a gun, with great force.

I wasn't done yet, as I yanked my cock from her swollen, loving lips, and still grasping her by her dark reddish-brown hair, squirted the generous last of my cum all over her pretty, tan face.

"Ah!" was all she could say.

She flinched, like I was spitting or pissing on her, which, in actual fact, I suppose I was. I just didn't use my mouth or my hot piss.

Fuck, she was gonna hate me after this. I've protected her yet have always treated her as an adult, as much as I could without burning away all her childhood on things she didn't need to be concerned with, yet. Well, "yet" was now. She'd asked for something without a clue of what it would truly be like.

Not stories from her fast-tailed little friends, not watching her nasty little boyfriends do nasty things to other girls she didn't like.

Things she'd personally asked me to do, to her.

She'd hate me now for it; for putting a hot load of cum on her beautiful, poreless skin, and I wiped my cock on her cheek and chin, leaving the last of my cum. But, in cold fairness, she'd found it funny for Amy to get a cream pie face and besides I'd have the image of my Laila marked in my mind forever, regardless of her anger.

I let her go and took a step back and sat on the bed, my dick still in my hand and watched her, for her reaction.

Laila took my cock out of my hand, leaned to me, and eyes closed hard sucked the tip dry of any fresh cum left in it. Then snaked her little tongue over my hole, making my balls draw up to give more, but I was empty.

"Do that again, cock serpent."

She smiled, face full of cum spit, and did it again, before going to the mirror to see how my jizz facial looked on her. She ate most of it and the rest she smeared into her beautiful face.

My hot cream.

Not Yune's.

Not Tibby's.

I shouldn't take pride in it, but frankly I do.

* * * *

It was getting late; it'd be time for church. Or maybe we'd sleep in. I rubbed my empty balls and knew which choice I'd take there.

"Wash your face, brush your teeth, and get to bed. I'll be right back up." No pun intended.

I slipped on my white robe and double checked the doors and locks, like I do every night, and went out a second to move something on the front lawn; waved at Alida on her porch. I came in, locked up, washed my hands, and found my tired little girl asleep, in my bed, as naked as she'd been when the day'd started.

She'd missed a splatter of cum on her chin and on her sweet, relaxed walnut brown tit.

It was too tempting.

By the way, if you want someone else to swallow your cum, like it's ice cream, maybe you should taste it yourself, to see if it's appetizing in the least. Drinking lots of fruit juice makes it sweet. Eating lots of meat, drinking bitters, and smoking doesn't. My baby likes sweets and drank my full load, like it was cream soda, except what I washed her face in.

I sucked her brown titty clean, as it hardened against my tongue.

"Mm, Daddy. We're fucking again now?"

"Later, my sweet, baby girl. Go back to sleep."

I kissed her chin clean, too, and then turned off the light and slipped in naked next to her; my little kitten cuddled her soft cheek up on my grizzled chest, as I slipped my hand behind her, to cup that fine, round behind.

I slipped my hand between her asscheeks and fingered her little puckered hole, then licked her taste off my finger before slipping the wet digit deep into her tight, *tight* bunghole.

She didn't complain in her slumber; but, her round, brown buttocks pushed eagerly against my hand to have me inside her.

"M-Daddy," she said, as her little hand reached out, then clasped my cock and held me secure to her.

I reluctantly pulled my finger out her shithole and patted her round booty. Not tonight or tomorrow, but soon. My little student had a lot, yet, for me to teach her about cocks and pussy tricks, and *two* cocks . . . .

I squeezed her asscheek.

It'd be real soon for cherry number three, then four, and more.

The End.

Neale Sourna's
North Coast Academies' Diary
---
3 Sex Views: Ross, Laila, and Sascha *[16,337 words all 3 stories totaled]*

An Adult Fiction Compiled and Edited by

Neale Sourna

*Three (3) HUGE stories, **priced as ONE (1)!!***

(1.) Sascha; Laila's Classmate — Public Parking, Sex Squared *[8289 words]* **Studious, male teen virgin, Sascha, watches hottie valedictorian schoolmate Laila steam up her glasses, public sexin' her lucky stepdad, then nerdy Sasch "gets lucky," too, twice.**

(2.) Laila; Smarty Schoolgirl — Daddy's Willing Little Slut [3711 words] **Teen Laila's rape-punished by stepdaddy, Ross, for playing the skanking stepdaughter, and she loves it.**

(3.) Ross; Laila's Stepdad — My Daughter's Asshole Cherry [4337 words] **Daddy Ross regrets his criminal-rough treatment, until randy little Laila begs for more. And gets it.**

Graphic public sex and exhibitionism; voyeurism, teen male masturbation, virgin cock's *first* blowjob and *first* pussy fuck; *first* incest father-daughter rape *(willing)*, including *first* bare cock in vulnerable bare teen pussy, a volunteer cock suck thank you, before begging daddy for her *first* anal. And gets it.

ISBN 978-0-9796841-1-1
ISSN 1553-8656
Volume 3, Issue 1

3 Sex Views: Ross, Laila, and Sascha
by
Neale Sourna

1. Sascha; Laila's Classmate — Public Parking, Sex Squared *[8289 words]*

Yeah, I know. I'm such a dork.

I *always* get to my parking garage job, like, an hour early, so I hang in the far back stairwell, where I can do my homework or do just about anything; because few people park that far back that time of day, except on game evenings or opera nights, and I could, literally, stand there dick ass naked, in the "dead zone," for like an hour, writing my name in jack off, and no one'd see me; even though it's in public.

I told Laila that — *not about the jack off* — but about my little safe haven. I love how she listens, completely.

The big guys, who're in love with her, the so called "steaming hot guys," like the twins, fraternal, Tib and Tad, or Korean buck Yune don't get why she hangs with me.

She talks "to everyone who's interesting," that's what she said, Ms. Laila, with her gold, delicate wireframes eyeglasses, and tight little, Halle Berry-ish but prettier face and biracial tan-skinned body with that intense, round ass, at 104 lbs, *almost 5'3"*.

Laila is *the* hottest, smartest, I-really-want-to-fuck-her-brains-out girl in school, BUT her-berserker-giant-dad-WILL-castrate-me-to-the-bone.

"Oh, *that* girl," you say.

I mention this because, well, I'd gotten to work and I'd put aside my homework, the online 3D and pornographic, graphic novel I've been doing programmer notes for, and since, even though I may not have "the looks" or be classically cool or intimidatingly big or anything, except smart, I'm still a healthy guy with incendiary hormones, too.

But, don't cry for me, 'cause I got lucky, I mean *really, REALLY* lucky.

I was itching with all kinds of randiness, so I tossed the Advanced Calc back in the book bag and got my bony ass off my hard stairwell step to see what or who could be jerk off imagination material, like a lady changing her clothes from office suit to evening gown—*my favorite, until now*—as I looked out through the little glass window of the stairwell door into the garage, and….

Total score!!

This big, dark guy was parked center and back of the blind spot, we call the "dead zone," where my bosses are cheap and haven't fixed or replaced the security camera, which watches that lonely spot, and my empty, top stairwell, too.

Mr. Big and Dark, despite being this middle-aged guy, was a lucky, fucking stiff.

He sat in his fine car, still, looking like he had no plans to get out, 'cause he was quarter-turned toward the passenger side and spread out, relaxed, with one arm resting in the driver window and the other across the seat top, with his big head lolling back, but I could just see another small, dark head of some woman rhythmically bobbing up and down on him, in his lap.

God, what wouldn't I give to have a woman do *that* to me!

And because she wanted to, not 'cause I'd paid her.

Not that I've ever bought…!

He couldn't see me, so I watched through the safety glass, steaming it up, wishing I could see more over his big shoulder, and when he adjusted his situation and he gazed down all dreamy at his lover making love to his lap, with this amazed look on his face—.

It was Laila's dad! Ross Deever!

And I immediately bet myself that it was one of the horny school moms; or sex-starved teachers; or, more likely; a pussy-dripping, tartan-wearing, skank school chum of mine, breaking her jaw on that beast I saw on him at my other job, working the country club locker room.

All males are afraid to measure themselves up to him, and *all* the females at school, and out, drool over him!

Some call him the "Cavalier" or "Cowboy" or "Swashbuckler," behind his back, because he actually looks like a Hollywood picture perf-.

Fuck me!!

He'd shifted again, 'cause the woman sucking him off was driving him mad and setting him on fire, and then the car door popped open-.

Fuck me!!

It wasn't....

...just *some* woman, like the twin's skank MILF mom, and certainly not just some whorish schoolgirl from North Coast or from one of the public schools.

It was *Laila* herself, "resting her head in his lap," her *dad's* lap.

Okay, he's her *stepdad*, but he's the *only* dad she's ever had, since a baby, sucking her thumb.

That wasn't a thumb she was sucking now.

"Perfect Laila" has been my good friend, since we'd started advanced enrichment classes together; the smartest of the smart.

I was so startled and rattled, that I jumped back from the window, unable to look, but eventually *had* to, because hot Laila, the "Perfect Virgin," was sucking her dad's dick, and I wanted it to be *my* dick her strawberry pink lips sucked on.

And that *thing* of his is HUGE, and she's a small girl, but she didn't take that tiresome looking whopper of a thing out her mouth, as she pushed back her dark auburn hair off her perfect, tan-skinned face, pushed up her gold wireframe lenses, while stroking up and down his length, as she relentlessly kept sucking on that fat, dark monster of his, slipping wet and shiny through her overstretched lips.

In and out, in and out, like she was a pro.

A total profession teen whore, earning her pay, in a car park, sucking some horny, middle-aged guy's fucking huge....

Her *dad*!!!

Fuck me!!

Laila sucking cock, doing *that* head gesture, the "chicken neck" the guy's call it, when they boast about who and how long and how much some girl or someone's "MILF" mom enjoyed it as much as he did, with the "she" obviously made up, by most guys.

Except for Tib and Tad, those horn dog alphas don't have to lie.

Not Yune either, but he doesn't talk sex, but everyone knows he gets it.

Laila stopped sucking her dad off, to kiss and suck his fat balls, then to kiss and lick the huge, fat muffin top arrowhead of "it," like "it" was the sweetest tasting thing ever, then she ripped a packet open, and rolled a condom, the size of a fucking Baggie®, over him.

He shoved the seat back, for room, and she flipped up her herringbone plaid uniform skirt, high above vanilla wafer tan strong, dancer's thigh and round ass — *without any panties on!*

'cause I saw…everything — as Laila straddled her dad, and reached down between them, to put her big dad's big, huge dick where it'd do the most damage.

She wiggled and settled over it, until looking pleased with what she felt between her hot thighs, then seductively began sliding down on all that big, fat, dark and angry hard meat of Mr. Deever's, piercing up into her.

She's old enough, to give "consent," but she's so little, and she's still a teen, and probably with the tightest little virgin pussy to be had, 'cause her dad doesn't let her date, or fuck around — literally, but she was bouncing and sliding up and down, and still wiggling on Mr. Deever's fucking HUGE manhood!

You think, maybe Laila's not a virgin anymore?

Well, *obviously* "Virginal Laila" *wasn't a virgin*, not anymore, 'cause a cock *that* size, "swallowed" that fast, would rip a virgin pussy apart, but Laila took all of his thick, fat meat inside her.

Like she'd been doing it all the time.

Like as if she does <u>her dad</u> **all** the time.

Now, *that* thought nearly made my head explode. What else don't I know about her?

I did feel a *little* wrong, by watching, but let it wane, 'cause there was *so much more to see*.

I've watched Mr. Deever before, not at sex, but because he's fascinating, and because he's a smart but scary guy, a dangerous man, and more dangerous dad, who's overprotective of his sweet daughter and vigilant about keeping everyone out of her little panties.

But, she wasn't wearing them now, was she?

So, I watched big Mr. Deever watching his daughter, leisurely riding up and down on his cock, as she slowly opened her Peter Pan collared, virgin white school blouse for him, revealing a pure white, lacy bra.

In a few seconds, he'd expertly scooped her pert, little titties out of their cover, without taking the tit-sling loose, and was teasing mahogany brown aureoles with the black hairs of his thick mustache and goatee, then his hard, red tongue, after making the relaxed nipples tighten up fast for him, he began kissing and sucking on his own daughter's hard, brown little titties, with their perfect round, puffy areoles.

And, boy, did she *love* that.

"Laila has little girl's tits," a girl at school said repeatedly, until she got slapped by Laila's best friend, Alice.

Well, Laila wasn't acting very little girlish, she was cock whoring, like the teen girls in the videos I download; teasing and begging for it, for him to, well, do what he was doing.

This was so fucking outrageous!

Fucking another man's teenaged daughter was one thing, but fucking your own....

He is the coolest. Ever.

Tall and big Mr. Deever was all scrunched down, so he could lick and suck her cute little titties, as Laila seductively rode up and down on him, steadying herself with a palm on the car's ceiling, as she'd sometimes wiggle in place and he'd thrust up into her, all urgent and shit.

But I couldn't see as much of the *real contact* of their sexin', 'cause her stupid uniform skirt covered them.

But then, she laughed, all wicked and stuff, and I thought they were fighting, 'cause she jumped off him, accidentally hitting the horn, and jumped out of the car, disobeying him, as he called her to "get back in the car."

Then he commanded, which scared *me*, even through glass and door, but she refused each time.

No one refuses Mr. Deever.

He glanced around the public area, trying to be a little cautious, but Laila wasn't. She perched her fine, round behind on the front hood, with her little titties pointing out to the public and her school skirt pulled up, with her fine, ballet class legs open wide.

I saw Laila's pussy hair!

I'd always imagined it was a deep shade of dark auburn, but from here, it looked nearly as dark as his.

My view did confirm one thing, though, about what I'd once overheard some girls talking, after Phys Ed, all amazed, about how she still had "full hair, trimmed on the edges," but the *full* bush, not completely waxed bare like a doll, or hyper-manicured to little pussy mustaches, like most of the girls seemed to be doing.

Or so I've heard.

I wouldn't know, for sure, girls don't show me their pussies, with or without pubes, like they'd show Tibby and Tad, or Yune.

Well, fuck 'em.

What *those* guys wouldn't give to be *me*, right now, let alone Laila's stepdad.

Those girls had also whispered that Laila'd said that if Mr. Deever ever found out that she'd been "ripping" her hair out of "down th-there" he'd nervously stuttered, in full anxiety about his daughter's sexuality, he'd "punish" her for treating her body like she was "a cheap porn vixen."

Vixen, yes; cheap, no. There's nothing cheap about Laila.

And what *exactly* did Mr. Deever mean by "punish"?

Because the hottest, can't-touch girl in school was definitely slipping her dad the tight, wet pussy. But, then maybe the punishment for a cocklovin' teen whore was no more cock.

I really shouldn't think such things, about Laila, but it was happening *right before my eyes.*

Anyway, nobody'd believe me, if I told them *this*, and big Tib, the varsity football captain, and Yune, the varsity basketball captain, both all hard muscle, would bury the hatchet between them long

enough to pummel and bury me, for saying any such thing about Laila.

They both believe that *they're* Laila's man.

But my eyes weren't lying, and my cock ached sharply proving it.

And I laughed, because Mr. Deever was *her* man, and he'd beaten them all to it, to Laila's luscious, juicy pussy; with that cherry long gone.

Mr. Deever slicked his hand over his silver-speckled, crow dark hair and down that sinister silver and black face hair, sighed, and got out.

Fuck me!

His cock looked even bigger and longer, than before, standing erect from thick root to fat tip; looking positively ruthless. That monster of his was dark and full with lust, as he followed it to where she sat, wanting it.

Poor guy, I really feel he truly thought he might could pack up his hard peter, pull her skirt down, and get her randy schoolgirl ass back home for their incestuous lust fun, or punishment, or whatever, but clearly, his mind and his cock were in battle, and his cock was winning the war.

I knew a little of what he was up against. Laila'd, recently, pumped me for details about this place, after I said the stupid camera was still down, and she'd asked: *when it was empty, could anyone see, had I seen anyone doing anything risqué.*

Well, this was risky and naughty, sex with your dad, after school in a public garage; while your best lab partner watches you get it on.

I hoped with all my heart Mr. Deever didn't get a backbone, as hard as his cock and put her skirt down, and just leave.

I couldn't hear, but I saw her tease her dad, by waggling and shaking her puffy little titties, on her golden apple-sized breasts, before doing *really* naughty things with her tan little fingers, like slipping them around and then deep into her juicy pussy; her clean white short nails, then whole fingers disappearing to the last knuckle.

One finger, two fingers, three, and four, and….

Not something Valedictorians do, stick a fistful of fingers….

Laila might still make Valedictorian, but her "V" for virgin was *long* gone.

That's when I realized my hands were working my dick, which I'd mindlessly liberated, from trousers and underpants. I'd never get another opportunity to see *this*, probably.

Mr. Deever was strict about Laila, about her being out too late, and-.

Laila sniffed then licked, then sucked her shiny, little wet fingers clean of Laila pussy juice, before making a point of sloshing them around her wet cunt, again, reinserting them as deep in as they'd go between her brown thighs, completing the image of the perfect little teen whore, and again she pulled out shiny, wet fingers and presented them to Mr. Deever.

The *lucky* fucker!

What I wouldn't do to taste those musky, little fingers; I bet she's got a delicate flavor, too; first class girl, first class pussy.

He glanced around, looking like a sinister pirate or a bad Rottweiler, before sniffing, and then sucking her little, slick fingers, his tongue licking between her digits for every drop of her tasty, girl juice.

He went to her, as she pulled her hand back, so he'd come to her, and when he was close enough, I saw her reach with her other little greedy hand to grasp that huge, fat, condom covered meat club, which was too big for her to reach all around, but she guided its big fat mushroom head back into her pussy's tight little, still hungry mouth.

She'd had him before, in the car, but....

Despite knowing that, at first it looked like he'd totally *never* fit.

But, then Laila thrust her narrow hips up, and he pushed in, and this time, I could actually see *all* of Mr. Deever's huge, middle-aged cock abruptly go inside her, all the way up to his hairy, huge balls, ruthlessly stretching the ring of her glistening wet, hairy, little teen pussy wide, and I mean *wide*, around him....

She's such a *tiny* girl and he's so *big*, it looked like a pervy roughneck giant raping a dainty, little schoolgirl fairy; a *willing*, little schoolgirl fairy.

Hm. Wonder what that'd look like in 3D?

Her dad paused, and she watched him, while she pumped up on him, as he glanced around, at the public garage, listening to the usual sounds of squeaking tires somewhere distant.

Then, Mr. Deever took over the manual control of his joy stick and began *really* fucking her, as I saw the full span of that lengthy, fat monster repeatedly disappear into my former nap mate's barely 100 pound body.

And it was all so plain that she loved it, wanted it, and that I hadn't mistaken what had gone on before, beneath her perfectly dry-cleaned school skirt — *that she'd had that monster cock stuffed to the full, inside her sloppy wet hole.*

I rubbed my dry cock, spat on my hand for lubrication, but it wasn't enough for the job, so I made a quick backpack run to get the tube I carry, for when I'm bored with homework.

I ran back to the window, my dick firmly in slick grip, to see Ross "fucking dangerous" Deever going full tilt at little Laila's cock-stuffed cunt, while she was meeting him stroke for stroke, the whole car and her little titties jumping every time he pushed all that thick meat into her tight, slick orifice.

He grabbed her ankles and forced her ballet and Tai Chi loosened legs open, high and wide, to accommodate his big body between her young thighs, so he could get a better look at the nasty thing he was doing to his little girl — *totally destroying her tight, little, eager pussy.*

And, I *saw* everything…

…wondering how she took all of *that*, all of her huge dad inside her, without her "Daddy" splitting her juvenile cunt open, bursting her randy cunt apart with that thick beast and those huge, grizzle-black haired nads of his, banging against her tight asshole and round, brown asscheeks, pulverizing her good girl turned bad girl pussy to shreds.

And I intensely wished I could kneel close, at eye level and smell … Laila's *sex*, and *hot pussy*. Her incestuous, hot, dripping wet pussy.

What I wouldn't do, to fuck what he was fucking, just like he was fucking her, hard and demanding, like he totally owned her cock home.

Mr. Deever stared at Laila, like he was evil, as he fucked her, hard, and it was hot to watch, 'cause she looked the same. It was like he was all raping pirate gruff and saying to her:

"You want hard cock, bitch, don't yah, schoolgirl? Take all of your bad Daddy's middle-aged man's fat cock inside you, you whoring little teen cunt," and like she was saying back to him:

"I'm totally your cocksucking slut. Fuck me *harder*, Daddy, cum hard in me, mak—."

My mind froze there, my body completely on fire, as Mr. Deever banged his fatal cock faster in and out of her small body, with all this blistering hot urgency, and she wiggled around pumping her eager, hungry crotch in circular fucks, with his fat, hairy balls banging against her ass crack, which ran wet with hot slippery pussy juice dripping off her round brown asscheeks; *staining her uniform skirt with cunt wet.*

"Fuck her, man, fuck her," I chanted under my breath, fogging the window.

I wanted to fuck her so bad, as I worked the hell out of my dick, burning with rigid need, and—.

"Aaahhhmm!!!"

Fuck.

I was loud and hadn't meant to say a thing, when I came, especially not *that* loud, like that. I certainly didn't want *him* to hear or see me, but I couldn't stop cumming, and it was the hardest I'd ever....

Shush, idiot.

I was *trying* to be quiet.

There's not a guy in school who's not afraid of Mr. Ross Fucking Deever, whether boy or man, because *this* man *really* pounds steel with a hammer, making *real* swords for films and collectors and shit, and this man really knows how to *use* them.

He knows how to *hack* things, and people, to pieces.

I'd christened the door, squirted the entire contents of my bags; nothing new there, but I'd cum harder, spitting out more than I'd ever done before, like a fireman with a fire hose.

I was pretty fucking proud of myself.

I glanced back out at the Deevers and I'd missed a bit, he was done cumming — *He's definitely king of the cocks; deep, hard fucking and cumming, inside his own daughter.* — and Laila was still clutching to her big daddy, trembling, with this beatific and dreamy look on her face.

Fuck me.

I'd watched my good friend and lab partner Laila, the supposed "permanent virgin," and I'd *seen her cum* and now saw her pretty face in after cum glory with her dad's huge dick fully jammed inside her little body.

He rubbed up against her — *hard, hairy and fit belly against all smooth girliness* — and kissed her long and deep, with tongue, like a *lover*, not a loving father, then she threw her head back, arching her spine, and he couldn't resist her puffy, little titties and played with each with the tip of his tongue and softly bit her dark nips with his white teeth.

And she giggled, and sighed.

Then, as his big hand slid up her fine thigh and was cupping that very fine ass of hers — I don't know why — but, he abruptly looked directly at me, and I fucking froze, balls to brains turned to stone.

She looked too, in this lazy way, then I ducked back and didn't know what to do, except to quickly shove my suddenly limp dick away, and try to get my skinny ass out of there!

* * * *

I kept dropping shit.

I thought, "Fuck it, leave it, get it later."

But, even if Laila pretended she didn't recognize me, Mr. Deever'd find my stuff and *really* ID me, otherwise, I could deny it *was* me, who they saw; and who saw them.

I was so fucking screwed, either way.

The man makes long, sharp knives, for god's sake!

The garage door opened, quietly, behind me, and my pounding heart dropped, as my hairless scrotum drew up all the way to my constricted throat.

"Hey, perv."

I swallowed hard; it was just Laila, adjusting her wireframes over her large, root beer brown, intelligent eyes. Her pretty little, very modest and still scrumptious (*Is that too gay a word, but it's what they are.*), her scrumptious, little titties and breasts were back in her white lace bra, back inside her pristine white school blouse, when I slowly turned and hoped *he* wasn't there, too.

"Daddy's in the car, and pissed; at you, and me. I promised him no one would see us. And there you were."

"I work here! I *told* you I *always* do my homework and stuff, right here; where no one bothers me."

"Oh, maybe I forgot," she said in a voice and attitude that said she hadn't.

"You did *that* on purpose?" She got this wicked look in her eye.

"Fucked my daddy, 'on purpose'? Yeah, that was—."

"No, I-I … I mean. Fuck h-him, *knowing* I'd—?"

"Watch us? Yeah." She sniffed the air. "Smells like cum in here. Don't say I never gave you anything. Best show ever. You're the first to know, or to see us together, like that."

I didn't know what to say, *Thank you*?

She did a double take glance on my fresh cum splatter, which now was slowly sliding down, drying on the door. I thought she was going to say something about me marking my territory, but, instead, she said….

"And you're not telling anyone, Sascha. Now. Show me your cock."

What the fuck!

"You crazy? You're dad's like psycho, and huge. And right on the other side of that unlocked door!"

I glanced out, and he must've seen my movement because his big, dark head snapped around, his movement shaking the whole car, as if about to jump out, then he stopped and looked like he cursed, but I couldn't hear it. He stared straight ahead, to not see me, rubbed his hand down his beard and then seemed to be strangling the poor steering wheel's scrawny, teenaged neck.

He could do it, too, my neck or the car's. I've seen his hands up close; big, strong, deadly hands; the hands of a metalsmith aka blacksmith, not the hands of a PC programmer's, like my skinny, fragile dad's.

"You're *crazy*, Laila, your dad's right there, and he looks not just a bit pissed, but *really* pissed."

She waved a pretty little, natural nailed tan hand, then played with her dark red hair *(genetic color, not dye)* off her creamy, light caramel brown neck, and she looked sexy hot, radiating with after sex glow.

"He won't hurt you. I told him I'd handle it, that you're a reasonable boy. You know he likes you, Sasch. But he did change color when I palmed a condom outta my backpack, before coming your way. And he knew *exactly* what it was, by the sound or something."

She tilted her head, reciting, like she was telling some fairytale, that wouldn't get me killed; or castrated.

"Daddy asked," and she deepened her voice, " 'What's *that* for?' I told him 'an experiment' and 'Please, Daddy, let me handle Sascha, don't do anything, just wait here, I'll be back in a bit. It's just my Sascha.' And I came here with this."

She showed me the condom on her palm; it wasn't rubber, because she's allergic to latex. I've know that a long time, but knowing *that* has a whole new meaning now.

She smiled all sweet and bright-eyed behind the gold wireframes.

"Come on, Sasch, you've seen mine, little tittie top and furry-cum-fuck-me-*down*-here bottom; show me your cock. Or aren't we friends anymore, since you spied on me sucking and fucking my dad in public, like a common little teen whore, on her knees in a dirty back ally sex scene?"

That last part she said while sounding real sexy and teasing, stepping towards me; and my entire body flushed with this incredible heat and an even more incredible and sharp want, deep in my scrawny bags.

And my brain *screamed*, "Are you fucking crazy, dude?"

Laila waited and I watched the window of the door for her huge dad, then glanced down the empty, silent and hard staircase, before I fumbled and undid my fly and pulled out my re-stiffening meat; more lunch snack than Deever porterhouse.

Not even half as much as his, especially when he was erect like some fucking, super huge LOTR Grond© of a battering ram, with heavy ramming capabilities.

Fuck "Lord of the Rings," this is real.

And then there's my dick, really. Go on laugh, I've taken Phys Ed; I've heard it all.

"It's-It's not as much as his. Your dad is like a freak. I'm surprised you can walk; the way he battered the hell out of your cu —."

I stopped, abruptly; it was one thing to say those words in my head, or to whisper them, as I rubbed myself, but not in front....

Laila's eyes went wide.

"No. Say it, Sascha, I wantta hear you say it."

I could tell by her voice and look that she wanted it, well, nasty. We say all kinds of shit, out of earshot of her dad, but nothing like this. I could barely breathe; my heart was pounding so hard.

"The way he battered your nasty, little, dripping cunt all to hell. Your eager, sloppy wet cunt."

She liked the profanity, as she evaluated my slim offering, lying exposed to her view, making my mind stutter.

Laila's the best, though, she and Alice — *well, because Laila won't allow it* — never laugh at me, like the guys always do, and she was *looking* at me, now, at my dick, evaluating it.

Then, I got seriously nervous 'cause it'd relaxed, after I'd cum, and then it'd become hard-ish when I took it out for her, but now, under perfect Laila's scrutiny, and in memory that her middle-aged, hard-bodied, Lord of Swords, warrior dad had just fucked her brainless and bowlegged, even making her cum; my so-called "cock," my softening, Vienna sausage was trying to recede up to my belly button, to hide its pitiful state.

"Here, let me," she said softly, stepping closer, to touch me, touching my prick with the wonderful, gentle stroke of her fingertips.

"Laila, no," I said, not even convincing myself.

No wonder her dad was dick mad for her, and all I'd gotten was a few, tickling strokes on my bare flesh, but it was enough.

Laila, the queen of North Coast Academies was looking at *my* dick, and stroking *my* dick, petting *my* dick, and handling *my* dick; like she was getting to know a happy new pet, as all the hot blood in my body rushed to be of service to any and all desires of her greedy little fingers, and of Laila's needs.

Damn.

I hoped she *needed*, me, and that her dad, Mr. "Conan the Usurper©" would stay put, while I *tried* to be of service.

Her warm hand let go of me, a few long moments, as she went to check up on Mr. Deever, and I stood there with my dick hanging out, caught in between, as desire was making it hard, and anxiety was making it soft; either way, evidently, her dad was where she wanted him, and she came back and abruptly kneeled, right there, in my public, private stairwell, right in front of me, completely shocking me.

Yes, I know, you don't have to tell me. I'm such a dork, and a loser, and I don't know why I said it, but....

"No, Laila, don't."

Who else says polite and PC things, when a dream come true kneels to blow you?

Laila, as usual, didn't listen to me, thank god. Anyone who knows her well knows that when she really wants to do something, it's done; she may not say, "No," to your face, but she'll go and do it anyway.

She took my dick into her little hand, and she held all of me enslaved, as she tenderly fingered and stroked my tender, exposed dick head, like she was an expert, who'd been doing it for a thousand guys, on her teenaged, schoolgirl knees, in a thousand public parking lots...

...her young, teen throat coated from berry-colored full lips to full stomach with hot cum from a thousand different men.

My mind separated, following various trails of sensation, as I saw her both, in the real and through the reflection of me in her gold wire glasses, over her root beer browns, as Laila's rose pink tongue daintily licked the cock hole I pee with and jack off through, to send a huge shiver through me, like I was her warm ice cream cone, burning up.

I felt a slight pressure release, or more like her hot tongue and sweet, sucking and kissing lips were a magnet, pulling my cream from me, as I precummed for Laila, and my legs trembled.

Her little pink tongue flicked out so fast to taste my eager cum that I didn't feel it; and I was disappointed; she wouldn't want more of me, now.

"Hm," that was all she said, in a tone that was uncommitted, triggering the whining voice in my overheating head that confirmed she'd not want more, had just tasted *"boy cum"* and was done with me, after she'd tasted and had a man.

And then my spineless whine *argued about me*, being "inadequate, and *argued with me* about not wanting her to stop, despite feeling that "getting head" wasn't all *that*, not as great as … as all the "cool" guys kept say — .

Laila licked, with the fullness of her tongue, that full cum drop of mine; *my* cum drop, straight from the source, right off the "bone," and my knees nearly collapsed.

She pushed me back to sit on the hard, stone step, and I plopped down, and sat still, my knees wide, while Laila Mariah Deever, valedictorian frontrunner of our class, pushed her wireframe glasses up her cute nose and gave nerd king me, and valedictorian second, or third, runner up (*depending on Korean Amy, who's wasting her love being in love with Yune, who loves Laila, who was giving me…*), a blow job.

A real, fucking blow job; my first.

Laila's gorgeous head of wavy, shoulder length, medium dark auburn hair bobbed up and down, and *my dick* was in *her* mouth, and I finally *felt* how *fucking delicious* it FEELS to have *her* lick and suck and mouth-fuck me out of my mind, with such wonderful lips, tongue, gentle teeth; yeah, *those* wonderful little hands on *my nads*, then *that* luscious mouth devouring my bags, devouring *me*.

I get it now. I fucking get it, now!

Finally, get why Tibby and Tad are always talking some shit about having their cocks and nads sucked and munched on by this or that person, both female and male. That their cocks taste so good, and that it feels so good to be sucked on, by a girl or even a guy, who's clueless about it, but....

I think that part, about guys, was a joke, but if—?

"Aaahhh!!"

Climax hit me, before I knew it was coming.

Fast. I *came*.

Blew my wad.

Came, in Laila's mouth.

Not that I could stop myself; but, well, wouldn't you? It's what she wanted, isn't it?

I came, hard and hot; squirting, again and again, into the humid confines of Laila's mouth, her berry-colored full lips sealed around my dick's head—*like I've seen her draw on a straw of a thick milkshake, if it had a knob.*

And then, she pulled me out, popping me from that orifice, with her wicked little hand milking and milking me, *squirting my cream into her open mouth,* onto her willing tongue, like teen sluts—*"new to cock and eager for more"*—do in the raunchy porn flicks I download; with teen sluts, who look the most like Laila that I can find.

Laila Deever, the hottest "virgin" cunt in school, smooshed my fresh cum around in her pretty mouth, tasting it, like those connoisseurs do wine, and then....

She swallowed.

Laila swallowed!

My cum.

All of it.

Like a fucking pro.

Should've been easy for her, she'd been sucking off and swallowing Ross Deever's monster dick, so mine was just tasty dessert, after his full course meal.

"Got anything else to drink, perv?" Now, she wanted an aperitif.

I stumbled, lightheaded, over to my bag and gave her my unopened bottle of cran-apple juice. She drank about half, like normal, except the lips and tongue she'd placed on *this* bottle had just been sucking my dick completely inside out.

Laila licked her full lips, which were swollen from her cocksucking activities, and I tried to put my dick away, but she shook her head, meaning "no," and so I stood stark still, dick still out, as she took another peek out to be certain big dog Daddy Deever was staying where she'd told him to heel.

I hoped.

Hell, I was at heel.

Hell, I was at her beck and fucking call.

* * * *

We … *chatted*, like any day; about stupid teen and teacher shit at school, our Lit story problems, then about music, good and bad, and good and bad TV/film stuff; except I don't remember any more of that, now. Only that my dick was *still* hanging out, exposed, and that she was *still* Laila, the hottest girl in school, and completely not known as the sluttiest cunt in school, until now.

Because I now knew she was her Dad's Slutting Cunt, at home.

I wanted to ask and couldn't, and didn't, but she told me, anyway—*she often does*—told me, not handsome and steady Yune or dramatic and "gorgeous" Tad or his Neanderthug frat twin Tib.

Laila'd never sucked any of them off.

That I heard clear and remembered.

She touched my dick every now and then, evidently waiting for me to be ready. It didn't take long, I'm a teen, I'm *always* ready, let alone when a hot A-list girl's impatiently waiting, for *me*, to *have me*!

Then, I promptly did and said something stupid and self-deprecating, when I told her that "if the condom's one of [her] dad's, it'd slip completely off me."

Gratefully, she only smiled and didn't guffaw, and laugh to tears, as she can when she's *really* "tickled"; she kind of shyly said the non-rubber rubber was *hers*, not Mr. Deever's.

But, despite that, it didn't take long before she'd toughened up again and slipped her condom on me, her small hand and fingers driving me crazy, before she pushed me to sit, then squatted over and slipped me into her.

The flesh walls of her inside were slick and surprisingly hot and tight, as I sat still where I did my homework and she rode up and down on me, face to face, like she'd done with him, a cowgirl fully in charge, as I felt my cock fatten up and lengthen like never before, and I moved up inside her, like he'd done, filling her.

Laila's pussy; I was fucking *Laila*, or she was fucking me, it didn't fucking matter which.

But, then she abruptly stopped riding, and I thought maybe I wasn't filling enough, after her dad's horse cock; then I hoped that maybe she would kiss me, but she didn't and, instead, she took out those magnificent little titties of hers and let me have them, as she wiggled in my lap and smooshed around on my dick.

God, that *felt so good*, crotch to crotch, *my* dick deep inside of *her*, inside my hot Laila's hot, wet pussy.

Pounding and thrusting is good, but just smooshing and grinding in a tight, wet, hot pussy is good stuff, good fucking times; then she whispered to me, commanded me.

"Change position, Sascha."

Yeah, fucking whatever, just as long as that includes my fat dick in your hot, wet pussy, is what I thought, but didn't have the nerve to say, but she's known my thoughts before, why not now?

She smiled, smirked really, as we shifted around, and she reversed the cowgirl, presenting that incredible, delicious brown ass to me, as I held her and watched my fat dick disappear and reappear into the heart shape of her backside, as we fucked.

Fantastic. Fucking fantastic.

Then, it got *more* fantastic, when she gave me a dream fuck, like in the movies; up against the wall, her brown thighs open for me, as she pulled me to her, belly to belly, her school kilt pulled up, the fabric crushed between us, and she guided me, after I fumbled, unable to relocate her slippery vagina.

I slipped inside her, and….

We fucked, against the cinderblock wall.

I fucked Laila, her puffy, little titties jiggling, then squishing against my school dress shirt, as I held her tight against me, between hard me and the stone wall, as I fucked her little pussy and she fucked back, humping on my hard, needy dick.

I surprised her, when I pulled back to shallow fuck a while, staring down between us, staring at *my* cock not Yune's, Tad's, or Tib's — *All three with cocks closer to Mr. D's than mine. I hate phys ed!*

But it was *my* skinny, fat dick, covered with Laila's pussy juice, sliding and disappearing into Laila's fantastic hole of paradise.

Yeah, paradise, surrounding me with a dark swirl of deep auburn curls that felt like cool silk against my burning crotch.

And, best yet, despite having had that monster freak of a Godzilla® dad cock in her tight little pussy before I had her, she wasn't all stretched out, like a sock.

Laila giggled in my ear, and hugged me tight to her.

And Laila *did things*, deep inside her, like getting tighter, and grasping me, her pussy sucking on me, opening, then tightening up again and grasping again on me, sucking again on me, as I stopped thinking and became thoughtless feeling — *The Zen of fucking?*

I, me, Sascha the geek the nerd the dweeb, fucked Laila's eager pussy, making her pant and sigh in *my* ear, for me, and *my* happy, freakin' dick.

If asked ten minutes before, I'd've said that being blown was the best thing in the universe, I was wrong, fucking pussy is, and *always* will be.

Laila was fucking my mind completely, totally straight outta my head, straight out through my dick, like it was a fucking, fat straw, and my two swelling-to-pop balls were feeling the pressure and about to blow my brain, squirting across the room.

No, correction, squirting *into* her, *deep into Laila's* secret insides.

I'd never be valedictorian for sure now; hell, Laila could have all my brain smarts for this, 'cause....

Reading about fucking and feeling a fantastic cunt, fucking and squeezing and sucking your tool dry of nut juice, are two separate things, man.

Laila felt so damned wonderful, smelled even better, with that soft clean baby powder scent she wears now accented with *her* scent, hot and burning my mind, as it wafted up between us, mingling with my own.

She felt so damned fantastic, me fully inside of my goddess Laila, her glasses all steamed up, because of me, with her banging, sweet, mind-blowing, tight, little body banging against mine.

I held her tight against me, in my spindly arms, like I'd never let her go, our crotches met, and met again; as she took me inside her, letting me in her, in, in, in, in, i—.

I "blew my wad, again," as we sexually satisfied men say.

* * * *

Out of breath, seeing black and stars, I pushed hard into her, my asscheeks squeezed so tight together you'd never get a sheet of college rule paper between them, as my sweating nads completely drained of cum; emptied out into the now full condom's teat end.

But I imagined my hot was dangerously loose inside her, mingling with her tasty girl juices, where even Big Ross hadn't been.

I asked Laila if she'd cum, and'd climaxed too, 'cause I didn't wantta be selfish, but, face it, I'd all but blacked out, in a euphoric bliss of pussy drenched orgasm.

Or'd fallen into some fantasy's alternate universe.

Except that this wasn't a dream fantasy or sci-fi, it was *real* pussy, *real* sex, *real* orgasm *with a real girl.*

I snapped out of my pathetic self-involvement, before I missed something important of this special realness with her.

And with all that going through my mind and feelings, Laila hadn't answered me, so I manned up and asked again, in a whisper though, afraid of her answer.

"Laila? Did you cum?"

Oh, yeah, I was afraid, too, of asking if I'd been any good, as I then realized I'd seen Laila's most intimate face of pleasure, the one she'd had, flat on her back, with her huge dad fucking her bowlegged, masterfully battering her senseless with his huge, master cock, making her teen cum pour from her cunt, drooling its hot pussy juice, soaking her best school skirt, from all her dad's hard sexin'.

As she'd made that intimate, secret face and had cum, moaning and trembling in quakes.

Laila hadn't made a face or sound or shivered even close to that for me, and my amateur's....

She took off her smudged lenses from over her large dark brown eyes, smiled, and kissed me quick and soft on my lips, a little peck.

She's done that in front of the "boys," too. Almost got me killed the first time, until she'd made it clear that *she* could kiss *anyone* she wanted, and they'd have to take it; "little Laila's a total fucking ball breaker."

The guys've said so, behind her back, and I've always thought them crude and rude for saying so, and I've told them so, to their faces, and, instead of kicking my shit in, they've laughed at me, as if I didn't know a child's shit about the object of all our desires.

Well, now I know, as Laila Mariah Deever gave me the look she gives when she doesn't want to lie to me.

"I didn't cum. I don't cum all the time. No woman does." Except little Laila riding her big Daddy Ross' big fucking cock?

"You cum with him, *all* the time, don't'cha?" She rolled her eyes, not wanting to lie.

"O-kay. Yeah, I do. No lie, okay. But I couldn't help it just now, Sasch, I *wanted* to, with you. I liked it, with you. It was fun. You're good. I almost...."

She frowned, dark brows scrunched, in that thoughtful, smart girl, pretty girl way of hers, that she gets with someone she doesn't want to hurt, thinking that she's saying the wrong thing, and it's getting worse, because she's "too clever and sharp mouthed," as Ms. Finley-Brown in Lit says of her.

I saw the honesty light up Laila's enormous dark eyes, which seemed so close and so much more intimate and open to me, without the fragile framed glasses protecting them.

And then Laila began her first "dissatisfied-after-sex-with-a-boy" speech.

"Y'know, besides Daddy, Sascha, *you're* my first. Not Yune, not Tibby. Remember that, okay?"

"Why me? Just 'cause *I'm here*, or...?"

I don't know why I said that. I should've been nothing but grateful, and I was, but I was feeling used, and fucked over, and not in that good way, that we'd just done; as I still stood the closest I'd ever been to her, with my dick still held in her sweet....

Laila gave me that look of exasperation girls give certain guys, especially those they like, if not love.

"I'd never do *anything* like this by accident, or just because some boy's convenient, or.... I-I planned.... Truth, Sasch? Absolute? I wanted to see what'd be like with another guy, a boy I like, who's my age, and who's like me, new to it."

But, not as *new* as-.

"Yeah, that's me, 'Sascha, the virgin'."

"Not anymore, silly. And with *me*."

She said it without being full of herself; it was just the honest to god truth.

"I *trust* you, completely, Sascha, that's why.... I'm sorry you can't tell anyone, but I don't want anyone finding out about my dad, it might hurt his reputation. And kill his business. But, it might make his internet sales soar, though; those clients are ... *different.*

"And, Sascha, more important, and immediate, I don't want the boys at school hurting you. Yune might laugh it off, eventually, but Tibby won't, and Tad'll egg him on, just to start some shit."

When did she start cussing, I almost asked, but then, answered myself, when she'd first come through my parking stair door; she'd technically said things her dad'd forbade her to say; besides, she probably started cursing and saying things like "cum" and "fucking" etcetera when she started fucking her dad, and swallowing his hard, fat cock and eating his cum, so I didn't really want to go there.

I was getting pretty exhausted with revelations about my friend, and the "afterglow" hormones were making me a little dopey.

And besides, let 'em "start some shit," I didn't care, I was *still* inside Laila, until she moved, and I felt her release me, making my dick slither out from her perfect orifice, like a joy-filled, relaxed newborn.

She shoved her uniform skirt down in a manner that made me know before she said it, that we were done and that this was our one and only time; before she reinforced that I wasn't to say anything about her dad and her, or about her and me, and even took the used, "cream"-filled condom back, in a tissue, like it was confiscated evidence.

She kissed me on the cheek, so near my mouth, but not like she'd deep French Kissed him, lingering a little longer this time, just a bit, then the door clicked open and closed, and I was left there with my satiated dick out, covered with her clear cream, at it's root.

I wiped some off, smelled "Laila's cum"—something I'd never truly let myself think of, let alone ever expect to ever….

And then, I tasted Laila, as I heard the Deevers' car peel away.

I dimly wished and laughed that it was too bad I couldn't suck her taste off my own dick.

Laila.

Laila smelled and tasted delicate, and unforgettable; I wished I'd put my face between her brown thighs and eaten her ou-.

A staircase door burst open below and someone bellowed for me and my "skinny ass" to get my "fucking nose out of" my "(GD) books" and "get to the booth."

I manned up, for once, and yelled back my disgruntled, true feelings in the matter.

"Fuck you, Harry!"

There was a pause; I'd shocked him, and then I heard him answer, with an approving sound in his voice.

"Yeah? Well, whatever, S, just get your bony, smart ass down here! I got break."

I resituated my happily satisfied "equipment" and took my (GD) time about it; so I wouldn't be there before Mr. Deever, still all pissed black, drove through the gate for home, with Laila beside him.

2. Laila; Smarty Schoolgirl — Daddy's Willing Little Slut [3711 *words*]

My Daddy was not happy, not at all. I'd gotten him to take me to Sascha's particular parking garage, that he works in after school, and I'd surprised Daddy with sex, *great sex*, completely and *totally hot sex*, like I'd planned.

But then he'd realized that Sascha had seen us, just like I'd hoped, and somewhere in a more than halfway-planned, half-formed, half-hoped idea, that I let bloom in full, I'd begged my very angry Daddy to stay in the car, while I got out to "go, talk to Sascha."

I'd even been completely prepared.

Daddy'd seen me palm the condom, though, and he changed to the color of a raging storm, so I'd been *real* sweet and manipulative, to get him to stay in the car, because I didn't want him breaking Sascha's slender, unathletic neck; just for seeing me and Daddy together.

But, Daddy hadn't been happy about me going into the stairway alcove, either, with a "rubber" in my hand, like a street prostitute all ready and willing and giving away "a freebie," just like a little teen whore, who'd just sucked off and literally gotten off one cock, to suck and ride another.

Although I think, now, that Daddy must've felt that, but didn't think it through that clearly, knowing that if he did think, clearly, someone'd probably die, and it'd be my friend Sascha.

So he didn't think as, I left one guy to go "talk" to another, like that teen pro with her pussy still hot and well used and wet from the first cock, and already seeking a second.

LOL

What a slut I've become!

Since I'd seduced my sweet Dad into fucking me that first time, and for my coming of age gift to me, he'd felt me up and finger-fucked me, and ate me out, till I poured girl cum out into his mouth like a porn tart, before he'd taken my cunt cherry.

So, then, I'd finished with sweet Sascha and'd put my school skirt back down and buttoned my dress blouse back into proper place, despite my sexy parts and my inside thighs being all drippy slick humid from having not *one*, but *two* lovers fuck me, right behind each other!

What. A. Slut! :)

I put on a solemn and serious face and got in the car, and felt that *feeling* in my crotch you get from having had a full cock, well, two wonderful cocks fill you and stretch you inside, then leave you empty, but leave you still *feeling* them, especially when you sit on your sex.

"Buckle up," Daddy gruffed at me. I promptly buckled up.

He groaned when I put the tissue with the used condom wrapped in it in the little trash bag we keep in the car.

He glared at me a long time, and I tried my best to look as innocent and as much his beloved, little girl as I could, considering I smelled of sex with two different men, back to back, in a public car park, and didn't have a stitch on under my skirt, like a good, private schoolgirl should.

I made the mental note to not turn my back to him going in the house, or to remember cover my backside with my blazer or backpack, 'cause I was leaking wet, as I *felt* it run down out of me like happy tears, soaking my best school kilt with residual, after sex[2] pussy juice.

Daddy stared at my lap, and I wondered if maybe he was thinking something similar; but didn't ask, as we peeled off for home.

* * * *

Pretty Ms. Cross, Tib and Tad's mom, waved at us and I waved back. She looked concerned but shrugged, knowing my dad's moods well enough that if he were upset about something stupid I'd done, she'd not change his mind, not until he cooled down, and then, probably not even then.

My dad's totally old school about some things; so, we don't have an automatic garage opener. He lurched to park, jumped out, stalked to the garage door and manually lifted it—*Gosh, he's got great arms and … everything else.*—then he drove us inside.

We normally park in the drive.

He jumped out again, his body all hostile attitude, and the door came down, sealing us in, and then he immediately reached in the car and snatched the trash bag, tossing it into the large bin for trash day.

"In the house. Now!" he barked. "Go to your room; and *stay* there."

I did, but, to tell the truth, I was a little disappointed, I thought he'd do like in that movie he finally let me watch, where the couple had nasty hot sex in the garage, but he probably felt I'd had enough of *that*, for now.

"And wash; your hair, your *entire* body, you...."

He didn't finish *that* one, probably because he was clearly about to say something mean to me, his own little girl, or just something completely foul. Shame on him; and after all that lovely naughty talk he does in my ear when he's fucking me real deep and nasty with his fat thingy, like they say dad's shouldn't.

Well, I think they should, if the kid really wants it. And not "wants it," like those creepy old guys they arrest on TV always say. I wonder if there're any creepy dads or neighbor guys like that, at our school.

Hm, I'll throw that question out to the forum and other blog, someone'll know, and tell.

Anyway, I was good, though, the complete best, and did *exactly* as Daddy'd commanded. I washed hair, body, and thoroughly douched out my girly parts, as implied. Clean as a whistle, all squeaky clean. I was still damp everywhere, and I'd put on my fave, the pink chenille robe with the happy, teddy bear on it, and went back to my room.

It was completely dark outside, and the house was gloomy dark, too, like his mood.

I wasn't certain where he was.

I can usually tell or even hear him, if the door to the design studio-smith shop is open; but there was nothing, not *one* sound, not anywhere; which was kind of unnerving. I like having sound in the house; him working, or humming to himself, moving about, making homey sounds; even playing his seventies' tunes.

But, for now, he was clearly off, somewhere, sulking in silent darkness, until....

I was staring at my CDs, trying to figure out what to play, to fill the silence, or just to put on the mp3 player to cycle my usual, top rated faves, when Daddy, with a dark scowl on his face, strode in, entirely naked, with a full, thick hard on, and grabbed me, completely snatching my bare, little size sixes right off the floor, and in the air!

He's my sweet, overprotective dad, so I always forget how ginormous and dangerous he is, when upset, and what a temper he has. He was like a grizzly bear in my room, with me caught in his giant paws; vised in his grip.

Daddy forced me down on my cushy single bed, knocking the wind out of me.

It's a single 'cause he says I won't need more than that, for sleeping, because he's "*never* going to let [me] bring *any* of [my] *little* boyfriends home."

I fought him, but Daddy's stronger than me, Mr. Literally-Pounds-Metal-Almost-*Every*day. He's blacksmith strong, as we lay cattycornered, with me just plain cornered on my bed, and panting for breath, unable to free myself from his iron-strong grip.

His greater weight held me down, pushing me into the mattress, my pink robe open, with his nude, hairy and hard male body lying on top of mine.

Daddy held my slender wrists over my head in one large hand, before he forced my slender, round thighs open with his harder, hairier ones, and then he felt with his other hand between my clean, pussy lips.

He kissed me hard, without kindness, then forced his tongue in my mouth, as his fingers rudely assaulted my freshly cleansed, girl sex parts, in search of ready moisture, which came not long after he stared me in the eye, like a dare to scream, before bowing his head down to my sensitive nipple, to roughly circle his pink tongue around my walnut brown areole, making my tit harden and stand tall for him, and then he gnawed on it.

And it felt like my entire body was suddenly in my breast, in that needy tittie in his vicious, hot mouth.

"Oh, Daddy."

I drenched his fingers, with liquid lust, right at that moment, and he grunted with the satisfaction of controlling my body, as I tired of wiggling to be free, and couldn't be, didn't want to be.

So, I went limp, unable to escape him, waiting, as he continued sucking and gnawing ruthlessly on my tittie, and fingering my cunt with his long, thick digits, massaging my clit, while pushing his fingers inside me, too, up to the last knuckle, fingerfucking me, driving me insane, until he removed them long enough to suck my hot sex juice off his drenched fingers.

He was distracted, so I wiggled out like a rabbit and tried to run, but he'd anticipated and grabbed me with one hand, while the other ripped my robe off, out of his way.

Then, Daddy pinned my naked ass down on the smooth, cold wood floor with his body weight, his hairy naked skin on my smooth naked skin, as he placed me on my back, then repinned my arms in bondage overhead.

I couldn't miss *it*, not seeing it, or feeling it, as *it* fell hard and heavy, thudding against my belly and then below, as Daddy resituated himself.

It was shiny hard, and thicker than my wrist, and he pushed it down between my tan thighs, his hard knuckles bruising into my tender flesh, before Daddy, without his usual kindness and care, rudely shoved his thick, long cock to the hilt in my wet pussy, ready or not.

"Ahhm," he sighed, sounding obviously pleased with what he felt.

The force of his cruel thrust pushed me, sliding a bit away, across the wood floor against my backside, but he roughly pulled me back beneath him, forcing my thighs wide with his thick body, completely filling me, till I was stuffed full with Daddy's lust; seeming like having a wide telephone pole wedged inside the tender core of me; a throbbing, thrusting, alive "wood" pole.

At least he'd made my pussy wet, instead of forcing me dry from the bath, that would've ripped me open, completely hurting and tearing me apart.

That's disgusting, and wouldn't be fun for either of us.

Being a stupid, cruel animal, ripping apart its living plaything, forever ruining the joy.

End commentary.

My Daddy's not like th-.

Despite what he was doing to m-.

"M-Don't."

I moaned that, not really protesting about what he was doing, to me, as Daddy's huge sex organ, his magnificent thingy, his precious penis, his yummy fat cock, so much better educated than my "almost" virgin....

As he assaulted and abused my poor, dripping wet, little pu-.

Daddy didn't listen to my—*What?*—my sham protest, my pleading, begging plea for him to continue.

He didn't stop or slow anyway, and that was fine, 'cause I *really* didn't want him to.

Then, Daddy hissed in my ear, hotly telling me who and what I am.

"You fucking … heartless … little … whore. You're mine! Your tight little cunt's completely mine! *Only* mine."

Oh, my poor Daddy.

I'd abused his feelings, and he was punishing me, for playing the skank; reclaiming me, because I'm *his* whore, I'm my Daddy's eager, little, teen whore, and had only been *his* whore, since I'd given Daddy my virginity, my pussy cherry; until I'd given Sascha some fresh and ready cunt.

Daddy's so big, and strong, and intense.

It was so deliciously frightening!

And exciting!

Being pinned beneath Daddy's hard bodied lust!

And he has such a *great* body, everyone says so, and it's all mine.

Or, rather, I was all his, and his fine, mad cock's.

Daddy was mean, now, ruthless; as his cock fucked hard into me and hurt me, but I liked that it hurt.

He'd always been so careful and kind, never drawing blood, or truly hurting me, not even when he took my cherry, "deflowered" me, as the old folks say, and now he was an animal, a fucking animal,

literally, like that NIN song we both love, but he used to wouldn't let me listen to.

He even smelled like a hot, randy animal; still smelling of sex from before, with me, from before I'd taken Sascha between my whoring, cock-seeking, teen thighs.

Educating my friend Sascha was fun, but this, oh, this is, oh-mm...!

"Don't! Stop! Daddy!"

I *think* I said aloud. Or I may've been fucked speechless, except for an occasional "Ow!" or to whimper, 'cause he felt *so* delicious inside me, and against me; hot and wet and grinding me hard into the wood, with his hard "wood" wedged and thrusting inside....

Daddy was out of control of himself, but fully in control of me.

It was scary, 'cause I usually have control over my Daddy—*"wrapped around my little finger"*—most times, but not *this* time, as he positively pulverized my girly little teen pussy to pieces, with his huge, middle-aged man's cock; all hard and demanding, without "parental control."

Daddy, again, fucked my mouth with his own; his fat, hard tongue raping mine, while he thrust himself into the center of me, bruising me, inside and out.

As if to fully force his way, fat cock first, to enter me with his entire thick, muscle-hard body, with a relentless lack of mercy and selfish cruelty he'd never done to me before.

I loved it; *loved it*; LOVED IT!

Every cruel, hard thrust of my Daddy's.

Isn't that so perverse of me? But it's true.

Told yah. I'm my Daddy's little whore.

I couldn't move, 'cause he was so heavy on me, weighing me down, his belly hot and sweaty against mine, so all I could do was take what he gave, and he gave it, hard, ruthless thrust after ruthless thrust, filling and emptying me, in that special way a slender, tender shaft is filled and emptied by a thick, hard piston.

A fisting piston that stretched my cunt hole wide, nearly to breaking; with all that fantastic fat girth of Daddy's huge, rigid cock; its fat muffin head plunging deep in and out of me.

Driving me crazy. And wanton.

I couldn't get enough of him, as Daddy's large, prickly balls, all swollen and heavy, thumped against my bare bottom.

His hairy, sweaty chest scraped my baby-ish titties with each stiff ramming thrust into my depths.

And Daddy forced my knees even higher and wider, to accommodate the wild-charging, sex movements of his large, male body.

He huffed in my ear like a great, randy bull in hot, searing heat, and my cunt poured out its juices, like the drooling, insatiable, Daddy cock-hungry mouth it is.

I *am* a slut; I'm *his* whore, my Daddy's slutting whore, completely and always, as he murmured hot in my ear, like he was loosing his ability to speak.

"…exactly like … you want … skanking, fucking … baby whore."

My back arched, right then, with all this *crazy power* and *electricity* running through me, straight from Daddy's fat cock into my slop dripping cunt, as I-.

"AAhhuhh!!!"

I trembled and shuddered violently and came, all out of control, like my entire body was cumming, cunt to brain, cunt to toe tip.

And I managed some, uncontrolled, undignified, moaning grunt I'd never done before, in mammalian guttural approval of what my hot Daddy was doing, to me, ruining both me and my teen pussy for anyone else, as I felt the center of me both contract tight and yet fall away into an abyss, taking away any last control I might have, as my little cunt sucked hard on Daddy's hard cock.

I nearly passed out from cumming, because all I was, was hot, tight cunt, stuffed to overflow with Daddy's hard, demanding cock, and I was cumming and *cumming* so hard *for him* and *in spite of* and *because* of my Daddy's relentless, cruel mistreatment.

"Mm," he sighed deep, as he sealed my lips with his, and tongue-fucked my mouth, and shoved himself, full cock and completely deep, into the center of me, grinding his hot, swollen balls against me, his black and silver pubes biting my flesh, down there, where it's tenderest.

"Ahhh!!!"

Daddy's cock blew hard, shooting his scorching hot cum *deep* into my soul, *deep* into my teen cunt, which went mad, again, and contracted tight and grasped him and sucked hard and ceaselessly on him for *every* drop of lust and rage my Daddy had to give me, as he groaned from the core of him and pulsed and throbbed, as if he'd shoved his entire heart to overflowing, straight into the tight, wet confines of my slick and abused, little teenaged cunt.

There was this incredible throbbing, throbbing, throbbing which matched the pounding of his strong heart against my ravaged little tittie, until that wonderful pulse finally faded slowly away to a soft whisper that owned me, from inside out.

Oh, so delicious, "Mmm."

He lay on top of me, a long, long while, his hot belly breathing pushing out against mine, his fat cock still completely stuffed inside me, filling me to the brim with him, my thighs exhausted like a rag-doll's, as Daddy ground his demanding crotch against mine, savoring our connection, like he still wanted to be entirely inside of me; a sure sign I now know well.

My Daddy loves the feel of his cock inside me, of my cunt and body wrapped around his, holding him close to me, inside of me, and I wiggled back, all hot and slippery, all squishy and satisfied, and purred in his ear.

"That was *the best*, ever, Daddy. You can *rape* me, anytime, Daddy. Especially, *bare* cock in *bare* pussy. The *delicious* very best, ever! M-mm."

"Uh, fu-...," Daddy moaned, pathetically.

Then, after lying on top of me a while longer, he finally pulled his dwindling telephone pole out of my slurping pussy hole, and he looked at his beautiful cock, slick and shiny from wide head to hairy balls, with my glistening pussy juice *and* his delicious, creamy cum.

Daddy moaned, again, pathetically.

"Fuck! Fucking hell!" he cursed.

But I felt: "Yeah. *Exactly*. A totally *delicious* fuck."

Daddy abruptly got up and left my room, then came back in, just a half minute later, trying to get that big, bad man's bad cock back in his trousers. He stopped fumbling with it, and covered the opening with big hand, and abruptly halted, when he looked at me.

I still lay like a discarded and abused, little sex doll on the hard-wood floor, hair mussed, top and bottom, bruises on sore tailbone, wrists and between my sore, abused thighs and joints, with soaked pubes and my very sore little cunt; the center of my Daddy's worried attention.

I was happy; dribbling hot cum juice happy.

He stared at my rough-used cunt, between my still wide open, tender thighs a long while, then he finally looked away, before forcing himself to face my face.

"I-I-I'm s-sorry, b-baby. I-I sh-shouldn't've…. Better douche my … *cum* … out. Don't lie on your back, like that, my cum'll…! You hear me, Laila? You'll … d-douche? Promise me?"

I thought: "What? Douche? Again?!"

I sat up, to hold my knees, once I could close my sore-jointed thighs, and felt how totally sore I was all over, especially deep inside my cunt, from my hairy little pussy lips to my secret cervix deep inside.

It did occur to me, just then, that what he'd done to me, I'd probably not like at all, if a stranger or someone I knew but hadn't wanted them….

Then, again, maybe I'm one of those, who do like it, no matter who…?

I don't think so. Do you?

Anyway, I know it seems just academic, mental stuff what I'm thinking, and lots of people would say something nasty, like, "You wait till you're raped, for real, you smart-assed, little bitch."

Well, that's not a nice thing to wish a person.

But, on the other hand, what I did to Sasch, because he'd never say no to me, wasn't that rape too?

Or just seduction?

Or, he's a guy and wants "it" all the time; especially, when it's not a fat dick up *his* skinny ass, or down *his* slender throat. Guys and *their* hormones.

Well, I'm a horny teenaged girl and I want "it," too; at least from Daddy.

No, I'm certain, that my Daddy taking me like that and holding me down and ... some girls *wouldn't* like that, but I did and it was because it was someone I love much and who loves me, unquestioningly; giving a thing, normally called negative, so much positive and wonderful power over me, and inside me.

Basic complicated human math. :)

"Laila?"

My Daddy was still waiting.

I nodded then, because he'd kept waiting for an answer and because my sweet Daddy looked *so* positively upset with what he'd done to me, so I promised.

He looked relieved, but still guilty and unhappy, yet relieved a little, apparently.

And then he abruptly went to his room, shutting his door, and soon afterward I heard him showering, for a long, long time.

I did get my bag for douching, but with the short nozzle.

Then, I only ran the water and made the noises, pretending to do what he said; but, I left my Daddy's yummy hot cum right where it'd be safest, right where Daddy'd squirted and deposited it himself; deep, Daddy deep and no return, in my hot, all slippery wet, and swollen sore, teen cunt.

But I made my preparations for Daddy, 'cause I wanted more....

3. Ross; Laila's Stepdad — My Daughter's Asshole Cherry *[4337 words]*

"I am fucking losing my mind! What the fuck have I done, *now!*"

I was standing in my bedroom, having scalded myself in hot water, again, to scorch away my sins, again, and cold water, again, to remind me to cool my lust to ice, with a vulnerable, teenaged daughter in my charge.

And I feared, but was certain, in fact, that it hadn't worked. Again.

I stood in front of my full length mirror, white terry cloth robe open and stared at my deadliest weapon of choice — *my cock lying benign and relaxed, having satiated himself, having satiated me-.*

"I *raped* her. *I raped my little Laila.* What the fuck is wrong with you!" I said to the incestuous rapist looking back from my mirror.

R-Raped her.

All because *she let that fucking, skinny, little Sascha fuck her little pussy,* and god only knows what else she did with him, let him do to her, in a back stairwell, like a common little street whore; doing things I'd taught her to do, and do well, with a man's body.

And some primal part of me had said to remind the straying little, willful, and randy bitch whose fat cock brings her joy that makes her tremble, and whose fat cock could punish her and fuck her crippled.

"Fuck me!"

Laila knocked on my door.

I jumped, startled, and my heart stopped. What was I going to do? I closed my robe, for starts, as if its whiteness could whitewash my black soul of the sins I couldn't seem to stop committing, with and against and inside Laila's delici — .

I shook my head, trying to clear it, and didn't say anything, but she walked in anyway.

At least she wasn't still lying naked on her floor, thighs splayed wide; like a telephone pole had split her; nor was she wearing the little girl robe I'd ripped from her, leaving her naked to my "parental" abuse.

Unfortunately though, she was wearing some new ballet pink tee top and matching panties, that were pretty much gauze thin, as I saw

the dark outlines of her perfect aureoles I'd just bruised and gnawed, and the outline of her sweet little snatch I'd just destroyed.

My eyeless cock saw too, and twitched.

Okay, not so satiated.

Fuck me.

And fuck my little Laila, the whoring little cunt, who'd lain flat on her naked back in her room, with me wedged to the hairy balls inside her....

Point blank.

Laila's little pussy sucking hard, draining my nads completely empty of hot cum, as I'd....

Hadn't she...?

Fuck me.

I gotta get help, gotta turn myself in, or-.

"It's all right, Daddy."

Her mellow-toned voice startled me, despite or because of its sweetness and concern, or, more likely, because I was lost full in myself, and fully going insane.

"I'm okay, sore, but, really, Daddy, it was the *yummiest, what you did to me.* I couldn't move or fuck back, and you kept at me. I tried to pussy suck on you and hold you tight inside me, like we both like so much, but you were so ruthless and fucked me inside out.

"And I wanted more and *more* and *MORE* of you, Daddy, inside me, banging me to mush, in that fantastic and wild...."

I'd heard her — *Hadn't I?* — and thought:

"My god, I've corrupted her so much that she really is a cock-whore, whose pussy I could away give away to friends and sell to strangers, like I sell designer swords, in magazines and online.

"Headline — Dirty Old Fucks: 'My daughter's hot, teen pussy, loves it all! In every hole, and every way! The nastier the better! And, she cums ... for her daddy.' "

I squelched that heinous thought!!

"Laila, you.... You should.... You can call the cops...."

But my nasty thought remained, not fully dying, as the thought of the Law died on my lips, because my little girl had this look of adulation on her young face, taking my breath away, when she actually knelt before me and ripped open my robe, exposing my "ruthless" and "deadly weapon of chose," hanging dangerously close before her flawless, young face.

Laila smiled up at me, then lovingly kissed my cock's resting head, tenderly licked her rose pink serpent of a tongue around it, to send delicious shivers up my spine and straight to my balls, before she drew the fat width of me inside her warm mouth and began sucking on me.

I was sore, too, from you know what, but my horny little daughter's sweet mouth was soft and wonderful.

And I felt myself falling into the trap of her-.

Again.

"Laila, no," I said, weakly, and tugged away, barely, from her, but she dug her white teeth in just enough, and *growled!* to say she meant business and that she wasn't letting me go, not just yet.

Of course, the vibration of that went through my sacs like fire.

So, I let my little girl take charge of me, because she wanted it, wanted me, and because I spoil her, by giving her what she wants, especially when it's a mouthful of *me* my Laila wants.

"That's it, baby, suck your daddy's...."

Damn, I love it to death, when she blows me.

I gazed downward between my hairy muscle hard thighs, at my little Laila, on her knees, with her stunning, poreless young face behind low reflection lenses and gold wireframes, loving my cock, with her beautiful little mouth; sucking the soreness away, turning softness into hardness, maddening me from balls to shaft to cockhead, and back again.

Her devoted tongue massaging me to the edge of cumming, until, postponing my ecstasy, she removed me from between her adoring, berry shaded lips and rubbing me, lust swollen, against her soft, peach round cheeks.

I was firm, aching, and wanting more.

"Don't stop, baby. Daddy loves…."

But the little bitch stopped, but held me enslaved with her gaze.

Laila stood and stepped back, so I could see her clearly, as she slipped the tight, gauzy tee above her little breasts, playing with them, as I played with my cock, waiting for her to tell me what she wanted of me next, where she wanted it next, in her throat, perhaps, 'cause I'd fucked the hell out of her pussy, but I'd fucked her cunt sore before, and she'd begged for more.

"What you want Daddy to do to you next, Baby? Show your Daddy."

Laila ran her hands down the front of her gauzy pants, through which I could see her dark pussy hair, then she slid her panties down, just enough, letting me see her beautiful, soft pubes without visual filter, before she turned, so I could see her panties just slide over the high, round double hillocks of her beautiful, tan brown buttocks, to make a ballet pink underscoring line of fabric beneath her two luscious and delicious loaves.

"Baby, you're driving me crazy. Where you want…? And how?"

She was revving me up, my belly and balls getting crazy, again; and I was trying to remember that as sore as my dick was, I'd just cockripped her apart, but, if she really wanted….

Laila bent all the way down, fantastic legs opening, as she presented her fine ass to me, doing a fine little stripper's take of taking off her little see through panties, to fling them in my face, leaving her completely bare, except for her wireframes, the little tee which'd fallen back down, and the delicate necklace she's worn since the first second I'd given it to her, a long time ago, for no other reason than for being a fantastic daughter, who loves her daddy, as she now pranced before me, showing off her sweet, eager assets.

"Oh, Baby, I want you so bad, but no, little Kitten, you're too sore, after…."

…me, *him*, and an *angry, ruthless me*, again. But, daaamn….

"No, Daddy," Laila giggled. "I have *another* cherry, see?"

She turned like she was modeling shorts, except that she was completely bare assed, and parted her high, plump, naked and brown asscheeks with her little fingers, like opening the halves of a delicious buttered bread roll, and I could see the reflection of the slick ass lube she'd squirted into her bowels, and that limned the tight meat ring circle of her welcoming little shithole with reflected light.

Like a goal; a fucking cock target.

Her last, unsavored, and untried cock ring hole of seduction and delight, in devotion to her beloved parent.

It'd fit me perfectly, once I reshaped it. And it spoke to me.

Slip me on, Daddy. Come on, Big Daddy, jam it in me.

My little girl wagged her ass back and forth; begging for my "thingy."

"Daddy, when you think I'm all asleep, you're always wetting your finger and sliding it in my asshole, and you *promised* you'd take *all* my three cherries.

"You took my cunt fuck cherry and my throat fuck cherry, now take my ass fuck cherry, tonight. Please? I can't wait any longer."

I *had* promised, but it sounded different, now, criminal even, coming from my little girl's beautiful lips, still wet and flushed from kissing and sucking my cock and balls.

Her mother'd fucking kill me, except the selfish bitch never comes home from her long distance, "powerful, glamour job," to suck and kiss my cock and balls.

But, that's no excuse for me.

Being alone with Laila, teaching her the things I was teaching her.

For god's sake, man, man up. You're her fucking dad, and….

"I-I just r-raped you, Kitten. Without a condom, I might could've put a baby in you. You should be turning me into the police."

"*No, Daddy,*" my little girl whined. "Finish the job. I begged you to do it in public and I sucked you and fucked you wild and nasty, like we both like."

Then she smiled, wicked, my sweet, little soon-to-be Valedictorian girl, as she illustrated with her lascivious, cock hungry little body.

"And then I sucked off Sascha, bare, and swallowed his hot cum, before cunt fucking him mad; first sitting, then up against the nasty wall," the little vile bitch said, with graphic determination to rile me, as the old folks would say.

"Then we get home, and you surprised me, totally, Daddy. *Raped* me, held me down and … m-yummy. I *loved* it. Totally. It was so completely sick!" she said, gleeful.

I wasn't imagining that, she was filled with glee, although her vernacular of "sick" threw me a moment, till remembering "sick" was like "bad," in certain contexts, it meant good, *really, divinely* good, or some such she'd explained to me once.

"It's okay, Daddy. I wouldn't want strange, mean men doing *that* to me, or a man I didn't love. And I don't have any homework to-night either. Fuck me some more, Daddy, fuck me in the ass, tonight, nice or rough. You want to, you know you do."

Yes, I did.

Okay, it may have been stupid to reason, but I'd taught her how to use her mind and reason and think things through, and so I held to that, just in case she was hepped up on hormones, or she was afraid of me, and this was what she thought would please me, so I wouldn't … something.

I couldn't think anymore, not with her pubes and booty and little ballet pink covered titties teasing me and begging me….

"Don't say that, Laila honey. You told me 'don't' earlier, and I didn't listen, Baby."

" 'Cause it was a *'Don't stop'* kind of *'don't.'* And *you* could tell. *Please,* Daddy, put that thick, long monster, Sascha's all afraid of and all envious about, in my ass, stuff me full with him and fuck me. *Please?* Assfuck me, Daddy. You've been wanting to, for so long. And your thick, fat cock's already all hard and long and ready."

She giggled, throaty and sexy.

"*That* fat, bad man between your legs wants *your* little baby's tight virgin shithole, doesn't he?"

She said *that* to *me*, as she lay back on my big bed and arched her back, pulling that little see through, gauzy shirt up, presenting her sweet, puffy, little titties, shaking them, and then presented me a magnificent view of her abused little, battered sore pussy.

And I swear I saw a trickle of undiluted Daddy cum roll out and down towards her asshole, as she pulled up her knees, then parted her tight asscheeks, to give me another fantastic look at the slick bit of virgin tail she was offering me.

My smart, little Laila's such a fucking cockloving, Daddy's whore.

She'd teased and given me so much pleasure, begging for it in the open, with her thighs opened wide on top of the car, and again when I'd thrown her on the floor and forced her.

She was right, she'd enjoyed it, I'd startled her at first, but then she'd mewed and wiggled and her begging pleas hadn't been at all for me to *stop* fucking her, to *stop* raping her little cunt to shreds, but to fuck her harder and….

What is a man supposed to do?

What's a dad to do, when his sweet, little baby slut pleads like that?

I felt a hard pull in my belly for that slick virgin asshole and my lusting cock and balls answered with a resounding, *give the little, insatiable bitch what she wants, the whore wants cock*; her very own middle-aged daddy's thick, fat, real man's cock meat, stuffed to the hairy nuts in her tight, teenaged, virgin shithole.

My Laila's a total Daddy's Girl, everyone says so; they have no fucking idea.

"Fuck me, Daddy," my Kitten purred.

And I do, as my hot, little bitch commands.

I dropped my robe and climbed into bed on top of her, naked again, in my bed, flesh to flesh, our skin colors, as always, contrasting nicely. My own little whoregirl, sometimes choirgirl, my little, pink ballerina, and I paused, thinking reasonably for a moment of her birth certificate without a father's name and the adoption papers I'd willingly signed so long ago, and smiled now, remembering those official paper's of authority over and possession of Laila.

Stepfather, not father.

Fuck, it didn't matter; stepdad or dad, legal or not; not the way Laila made my balls ache and burn to fuck her, and pleaded me to ream her virgin tight, teen ass.

My baby Laila always gets what she really wants, even if it's her daddy's big, fat dick in her tight, little wet twat, deep in her little vibrating throat, or all the way to the hilt, in her puckered little....

"Yeah, baby girl, Daddy's gonna bust you wide, little girl."

I stared between her thighs at her fucked up little raw pussy, kissed it gently and gave her a thrust of my tongue, making her flinched, and hiss with the pain, then licked around her pussy hole, before I put my thick cock to her shiny little shithole, swished its fat head around in the slick of the thick lube, and pushed.

No need for extended foreplay, she's been horny all day, since before school let out, and she'd invited me to a public garage, without her panties on, so she could take cock after cock.

I know my little slut of a cocksucking daughter; she'd known skinny Sasch'd be there.

Her tight, puckered hole resisted me; that's what you get when you fuck a virgin; even one who begs for it.

"You said you wanted your daddy's cock, whore, so open wide, and take it."

Laila, my sweet overachiever, took a breath and I felt her belly tense with her concentration, but her incredible buttocks and tight sphincter relaxed, as she opened herself to me, making her virginal asshole's pink mouth cave open to my push; pucker hole yawning wide to swallow the spongy fat head of my cock.

Laila made a face and a little sound of surprise, to have such a large, hard, man's tool in her ass, going the "wrong" way.

So, I stayed inside her and let her get used to the feel of my thickness, of that great mass going inside her, as she held tight to me and I held her luscious, smooth body to mine, while she felt my intrusive cock's thickness shoving up her down chute.

I kissed her sweet lips, sucked on her tongue, then nibbled on her sore tit, while rubbing gently on her clit and sliding a finger or two or three or four into the cum slick that was her pussy; sore or not, its mine.

"Ahhm," she gasped, but didn't really complain about my large fingers inside her.

Laila can be sweet, but she's stubborn, too. I know my daughter.

The lying, little bitch clearly hadn't rinsed my cum from her too vulnerable teen cunt, like she promised, she'd humored me, and I should be pissed with her endangering her future, but … my fat and happy cock was in her tight ass, correcting another flaw of her virginity, and we could deal in the morning with her sin of lying to her father and of my sin of raping my own little girl barecocked, like a foul beast in full heat.

"Laila, you think Sascha'd like a punishing, fat, ass raping cock up his tight, little teen sphincter, too, or has he already been selling his skinny tail to pervert sports jocks at school and dirty old men on the Net."

She giggled, then tried to look serious, as she relaxed her bowel muscles, and I slid in deeper.

"Stop it, Daddy. Besides, that'd be 'Quen the wench,' not Sasch."

" 'Stop' this?" I said, and halted entering her, pulling out a bit.

"Not *this*! Sasc…," she murmured in a dreamy manner, feeling me sink deeper and deeper into the lube slicked muscles of her virgin tight ass, to further violate her sweet body, as if it were mine to do with as I pleased; which it is.

I repositioning her little body to suit my huge one and slid all the way to the sword hilt in her, and slid out and back in a few times to let her feel my cock's bare head against her inner walls and my balls bang up against her backside.

She tightened around me, grasping and getting a feel and trying, already, to drive me wild, as she learned yet another useful and new skill, while riding her beloved daddy's demanding, ass-splitting, wide cock.

"Love gettin' your tight little ass fucked, don't yah, Kitten?"

"Mmm-yes. M-yes," she murmured, barely able to talk.

The little bitch was getting the hang of ass-pleasing my cock, but I was the master yet, as I pulled all the way out, anticipating correctly that she'd complain, before I flipped her on her side, rejammed my cock between her plump, firm asscheeks, right back in her slick rectum, and then reached around and gave her a bonus, when I shoved several fingers in her sore little pussy.

"Ah-mm!"

That was all she said, in complaint, then held my hand against her bruised clit and sore mound, as my baby girl, Laila, bounced her delicious little tan body against mine, so she could get the full effect of being assfucked and fingerfucked, both at once, by her loving dad.

"Like it don't you, Baby?"

"M-hm."

She couldn't talk, she loved it so much.

I pinched her sore tit, the one I abused earlier, and again, she still didn't complain, she hissed in pain, then sighed with a delicious little moan, as I felt both her cunt and her asshole tighten on me, so I pinched again and again, to feel her grasp at me again and again, as I ruthlessly banged Laila's asshole, fucking her, hard, reshaping her nasty little shithole to fit my large, hard pleasure, making her body yield to mine once more.

She made little sounds of amazed pleasure.

"Oh, oh. Ooh-mm."

I lay down and hugged her tight to me, and continued claiming her body and lust, fucking away at my ever so willing daughter, in her last virgin hole.

But, with so many sex acts yet to learn and experience, with me, she was yet a virgin.

I banged against my Laila's round, brown asscheeks, watching them ripple in that delicious way a girl's ass jiggles when you pound her from behind, whether in her sloppy wet pussy or in her slippery tight shit chute, but most especially in the behind, from behind.

Laila abruptly made an incredible sound of urgent pleasure, and turned her head to mine beside hers.

"M-Daddy, kiss me, *now, please.*"

I obliged and kissed her, her tongue seeking mine, so I let off the nipple to hold her sweet mouth where I could do the most damage, and my fingers slid in and out of her dripping wet, sore pussy, in a circular way.

She likes it when I do that, and my middle-aged cock, hard and thick, and bare burst, shooting fresh hot cum into my sweet, little Laila's virgin bowels.

"M-yes, Daddy," she murmured, her mouth on mine.

She grabbed the back of my head to not lose our deep, tongue-fucking kiss, and to grind her delicious ass back against me, as I rammed my fingers all the way into her cunt, and sore or not, my little slut shuddered and came all over my hand in great gushes, as my knuckles inside her rubbed against the thin wall that separated them from my cock.

I pulled her closer, and gave one more long, throbbing, nad relieving, grunting squirt into her greedy, tight, teen ass, just like she'd begged and pleaded for me to do, as I massaged piss-wet, cunt juice and hour-old Daddy cum around her swollen, hairy cunt lips.

My lying little dick slut; Daddy's lascivious, little cock whore.

And the fact that she'd wanted *my* horny, middle-aged, bare cock, and wanted *my* dangerous, plentiful cum deep inside her hot, dripping wet hole made my heart warm and my belly and balls ache, in trying to answer her siren's call, but my boys were already milked dry; in her sore pussy and in her reamed ass.

Yeah, I was finally dry, for now.

And I dimly toyed with whether I should allow her to wax hairless her sweet, eager, little pussy, like her friends at school do, or would that make her too much like when she was a real little kid; but it wouldn't really stop me, or her.

Besides, I like tugging on it and unveiling what's hidden to everyone, but me.

Not even Sasch; he didn't get a fuck-her-little-pussy-with-your-hard-tongue-till-she-cums-in-your-mouth taste of my little whore.

Laila reeked of musky sex, now, but just of me, not that damn, skinny kid, as I parted her asscheeks to watch as I slid in and out of her slick, firm, teen ass, with a guiding hand on my softening cock, and then pushed all the way back deep into her fully bored and stretched wide to the max asshole, to stay there, in her cozy hot bowels, as she took my hand from her sweet pussy and licked and sucked all our cum from my fingers.

A professional, little teen prostitute couldn't have done it better.

When done with her snack, my little girl became chatty; not usual for her.

"It's *so* yummy, Daddy, like having you fuck all the way up into my belly. You're so deep inside me."

She purred and half turned to look at me, with a question I already had an answer for.

"What're you gonna teach me *next*, Daddy?"

She looked so eager, innocent, and whorish all at once.

What was I going to teach my little overachiever next?

Easy.

I'd recently started letting her view my private DVDs and she'd become fascinated with my DP porn, that's why I tested her with both cock and fingers together, and she'd passed with flying colors.

What's next was simple, and inevitable; Double Penetration (DP) for my studious little schoolgirl.

I told her, and her large brown eyes grew even more huge with bright wonder and anticipated delight, behind the wireframes, at the next various ways she would be losing her DP virgin cherries.

Then she asked the next obvious question.

"But *who*, Daddy? Who'll you *let* fuck me? While *you* fuck me, *too? Who?* You *have* to tell me."

She was so excited, as I watched her and imagined my little Laila with two huge cocks inside her, at the same time; my little Laila pierced to the fat balls by two big, middle-aged men, fucking all their love into her; one with silver-grizzled black pubes, me; and one with silver-grizzled red pubes.

"Your Uncle Stan, Kitten. Would you like that? You've seen his big, mean cock, with all that red, curly hair at its base. You want your big Uncle Stan and his long, fat cock, don't you, little baby? In your pussy; stuffed deep down your throat; and in your nasty little shi-."

Laila squirmed in my arms with delight, distracting me.

She felt great against me, as I kissed her downy cheek and stroked her willing, naked body with my covetous hand, while she drifted off, pretty mouth fallen open.

I removed her wireframes and put them aside, as she dreamed of having her little teen body double-stuffed full with *two* incestuous, middle-aged, hard cocks, as my cock firmed up and grew thicker in her well-reamed, teenaged ass, satisfied; but wanting to spread out and keep possession of his new home.

And, Laila, in feeling me fill her, and stretch her, my sweet, little Laila sighed in contentment, while I gently fucked her, without goal, just because I could, until I, too, slept, contented; my fat cock still in her incredible, willing little brown ass.

The End.

More Incredible Fiction *[and nonfiction]* From Neale Sourna

At

www.Neale-Sourna.com

North Coast Academies' *http://north.neale-sourna.com*

www.PIE-Percept.com